VALENTINE MASQUERADE

New Year's Eve is hot and sultry in more ways than one when a tall, handsome prince fixes the newest lady in his court with a magnetic gaze. Who could say no to a prince — especially a charmer like Will Bradshaw? Caitlin has to wonder. And Will wonders, too, if he might have finally found the woman to banish the hurts of years gone by. But what if the one ill-judged mistake of Caitlin's past happens to be the single fault he can't accept?

MARGARET SUTHERLAND

VALENTINE MASQUERADE

Complete and Unabridged

LINFORD
Leicester

First published in Great Britain in 2014

First Linford Edition
published 2015

A catalogue record for this book is available from the British Library.

ISBN 978–1–4448–2264–9

Published by
F. A. Thorpe (Publishing)
Anstey, Leicestershire

Set by Words & Graphics Ltd.
Anstey, Leicestershire
Printed and bound in Great Britain by
T. J. International Ltd., Padstow, Cornwall

This book is printed on acid-free paper

Dedication

BEAU, the foster dog who came to stay

1

'You can look now.'

Heather turned her sister to face the long mirror, and wide sea-green eyes stared back at Caitlin. The slender figure might have stepped from a medieval tapestry. Waves of dark auburn hair framed her heart-shaped face and fell softly to her shoulders. The flowing white dress, drawn in under her neat bust by gold braid, would have suited a fairytale princess. Used to her work uniform, a nurse's plain and practical outfit, she hardly recognized the transformation.

Heather removed the last pin from the neckline of the graceful garment she'd improvised for Caitlin to wear to the New Year's Eve party . . . well, presumably a party. Heather and her husband Tony belonged to a group that celebrated the customs and fashions of the past. Heather had been sewing all the sultry afternoon, adding ribbons and braid to the costumes she and Tony and the two little girls planned to wear.

'I feel strange, dressed like this.' Caitlin slowly revolved, admiring the effect of the long gown. She was out of the habit of attending social occasions, and was struggling with the foreign heat of Sydney. A fortnight ago in Auckland, she'd still been wearing warm pajamas to bed.

'You look lovely.' Heather tugged at the shoulder line and stood back. 'But you're so slim, there's nothing to you!'

'For sure, the puppy fat's gone. I'm a big girl now.' Caitlin had no intention of explaining how last year's disastrous romance had taught her just how foolish and naïve she really was. Heather's appearance had changed, too. The heat and the demands of her young family were taking their toll.

'We'll soon put a few pounds back on you!'

As the older sister, Heather had

always taken care of her. This holiday would be a wonderful opportunity to catch up.

'I really do feel I belong in another time and place.' Caitlin brushed out the folds of her skirt. 'I want to walk and talk differently.'

Heather brushed lank blonde hair from her perspiring face. 'Some friends think we're crazy, dressing up, but that's just the feeling I get, too. Everyone adapts. The women are elegant. The men like chivalry and romance. No, it's true!' She laughed at her sister's look of disbelief. 'Courtesy and courtship are alive and well. Now excuse me, I'm going to change.'

As she left the room, Tony swept in, a swirl of cloak exposing his loose shirt, doublet and hose.

'My Lady Caitlin!'

He performed a gracious bow and she giggled, hardly able to associate this elegant courtier with her brother-in-law, who dressed in the baggy shorts and T-shirts of most Australian males enjoying their summer break. If only life was really like this! The married man who'd caused her such grief last year knew nothing of the art of romance. Even now, her stomach felt the clutch of misery, remembering Richard's self-pitying stories. She'd believed all the clichés, listened to all the promises, yet it had taken a year, and all her strength, to finally walk away.

'My lady looks thoughtful?'

'I'm just not sure what to expect tonight.'

Forgetting his pose, Tony gave her a brotherly hug. 'I guarantee you'll enjoy yourself. Tonight's the investiture of the new Prince of Lochac.'

Her enquiring expression led him to elaborate.

'We hold tourneys. Fighters compete for the title. Our prince gallantly won his title by force of arms.'

'You actually duel?'

Tony grinned. 'Wooden swords. We don't draw blood! Points are awarded for swordsmanship.'

'And who's this year's winner?'

'Will Bradshaw . . . ' Tony interrupted his reply, bending one knee and extending his hand as Heather returned. She'd changed her shabby shorts and top for a splendid dress of dark red silky material, full-skirted and low-cut. The neckline was set off by heavy metallic jewelry that looked as though it belonged in a royal vault. She laughed at Tony's posturing.

'It's only an old curtain, and the necklace is from Paddy's Market. What were you saying about Will?'

'Just filling Caitlin in on tonight's proceedings.'

'I hope you told her the new Prince of Lochac has a reputation as a heartbreaker.' She gave an odd laugh. 'Be warned, Caitlin!'

Tony disagreed. 'What rot. Will's too busy being an entrepreneur to have time for women.'

'That's not what the girls say.'

'Perhaps you pay too much attention to their gossip?'

Surprised by the sudden note of tension, Caitlin interrupted.

'You needn't worry about me, Heather. My heart's not available.'

'We'll see. Will's the archetypal tall, dark and handsome stranger.'

'I don't care what he is. I'm not interested.' She'd put her dreams away and had no intention of allowing any other man to storm her defenses and break her heart again.

Tony seemed intent on having the last word. 'Will's a damn good swordsman. When you see him in full dress tonight, you'll believe the twenty-first century is an illusion. He'll carry his crown justly. He's earned it.'

The two little girls ran in to show off their party wear. Tony swung each of them round and round while they squealed. He set them on their feet and stood back to admire their costumes, identical pale gold tunics with hand-woven belts.

'You've done a splendid job, love.' Tony hugged his wife as though soothing away the awkward moment, and she leaned against him, murmuring a soft apology.

Katy and Jackie ran to their aunt, tugging her by the hand to show her their crowns of imitation daisies. As Caitlin helped them thread the flowers in place, the touch of their soft skin and the scent of their silky blonde curls tugged at her heart. Heather's family ensured that, however constant the work, she could never know the pain of loneliness. Yet Caitlin doubted she could ever manage such responsibility.

'Will you girls look after me tonight?' Her nerves felt keyed-up. 'I've never been to a party like this. I won't know what to do.'

Her nieces were only too happy to help.

'You can sit at our table for the feast!'

'And we'll show you how to do the dances!'

'Then I'm sure to have a good time. Thank you.'

Heather looked on, enjoying the girls'

interaction with their aunt. 'Sometimes I wish we weren't living on opposite sides of the Tasman. Have you ever thought of migrating? A nurse can find work anywhere.'

'I've never thought about it.' That was true. Last year, her plans had revolved around Richard, marriage and perhaps a family down the track, once his divorce was absolute. Or so she'd believed. No, she had to steer her thoughts away from Richard. He was over, and she was through with men. Tonight's play-acting would be exactly that, and she would enjoy it for the game it was. The prospect of spending such an unusual night was starting to sound like fun. Old-fashioned courtesy might be a balm to her bruised heart. Dressing up was certainly a way of overcoming shyness. For a few hours she would be the Lady Caitlin, receptive to romance and charming overtures.

* * *

As Tony parked outside the hall, Caitlin half-expected to see horses tethered in the yard. No, the transport of the merrymakers was decidedly twenty-first century, and none too smart at that. Most cars looked ready for the trade-in department, apart from one low-slung Porsche.

'Our incoming prince's steed.' Tony sounded covetous, but she was unimpressed. She wanted more in a man than the wealth he might choose to display. Lifting the hem of her skirt above the summer dust, she followed Heather and the girls toward the entrance of an unimpressive hall. The paint was flaking and the building looked like the site of a scout meeting or country dance.

Inside, she drew an involuntary gasp. The change was miraculous. Candles sent fluttering shadows through the twilight, burnishing the metallic shields and suits of armor of two attendants who waited to receive new arrivals. Silken banners embroidered in fantastic designs swayed in the gentle breeze blowing through open windows. Men and women in gorgeous-hued dress stood in groups or glided among tables set with platters, goblets, old-fashioned spoons and large forks.

Tonight she could easily believe in time travel. Strolling players wove among the groups, making music with recorders, flutes and other instruments she was unfamiliar with; perhaps lutes or violas da gamba. She was greeted and introduced with courtly bows and gracious phrases of welcome that somehow inspired similar responses to trip from her tongue as though she'd been groomed for just such occasions. The atmosphere seemed to mask something significant; some important event that was about to touch and even change her. Alert, she sat quietly next to Heather on the wooden bench and drew her two nieces to sit on either side of her like small golden shields.

'Stay with me for a little while?'

The girls were content to sit and

stare at the activity, as members set up a mock throne and unfurled a roll of ruby carpet. Apparently the coronation was about to begin.

'Which one is going to be crowned?' she whispered, and her nieces stared around.

'That's the prince!' Jackie sounded awestruck. She was pointing to a tall figure, resplendent in a royal purple cape, who had just entered from a side door. Looking every inch a man who could carry a crown, he stood quietly, scanning the room. Draped cuffs fell gracefully over long hands as he gestured to various friends. Masculine boots set off muscular legs, confirming his strength and regal appearance.

'That's Will Bradshaw,' murmured Heather. 'I think he's seen the new lady in his court.'

For the prince, with measured steps, was advancing toward Caitlin, who sat like someone hypnotized as he bowed deeply, extending a hand toward her. Heather, who had risen to her feet, sank into a curtsey. Caitlin imitated her sister, surprised it felt quite natural. Will's hand held hers in light greeting as he enquired: 'My lady has traveled here from some far barony?'

Raising her green-eyed gaze to meet his penetrating blue eyes, she felt this physical meeting like a powerful surge of electricity. Entering into the game, she responded.

'Far indeed, sir. I have just recently crossed a sea to visit this land.'

A giddy sense of make-believe was pulling her into delicious fantasy, where codes of behavior were radically changed. A hot flush of excitement crept through her limbs as she held his look, refusing to break the contact. The prince spoke thoughtfully to Tony, who had hurried over to join Heather and his family.

'You have kept a treasure concealed within your household. But treasure should not be locked away. With your consent, perhaps I may acquaint our visitor with the charms of our shire during her stay?'

Not willing to be handed about like a parcel, Caitlin interrupted.

'Indeed, my liege, the ladies of my land decide on their own account with whom they dally.'

A flash of humor twitched at the corners of the prince's sensuous mouth.

'Your land is enlightened by all account. So then, my lady — will you dally with me?'

'In truth, sire, I cannot find it necessary to deny the wishes of a prince.'

'Well met!' Will was smiling at her demure reply. 'Courtiers summon me now and I must take my leave. A star shall shine on the hour of our meeting.'

He bowed and again Caitlin curtseyed, feeling the touch of his hand long after he'd walked to the coronation area.

'Caitlin, what a flirt you are!' Heather did not hide her surprise.

'It's just a game. You were right, it's fun!'

Heather did not look convinced. As a sudden trumpet fanfare silenced the gathering, she beckoned Caitlin to stand as a page stepped forward, unrolling a parchment scroll. He announced the coronation of the incoming prince, who was now walking the length of the red carpet toward his throne, accompanied by his court officials. His air of conviction almost denied this was only make-believe; his arresting presence radiated power. A tall, broad-shouldered figure, he towered over his retinue, the heeled boots adding to his stature, the candlelight dulling his costume so that he seemed clad in black robes surrounding him with mystery and authority.

He took the throne and the entire assembly bowed or curtseyed their acknowledgement. In pairs, they approached along the carpet to pay homage. As Caitlin's turn came, she felt like a true princess walking toward some fateful destiny. With gliding steps she reached the throne and curtseyed as was expected. To her surprise, the prince, who had merely acknowledged the others with a nod or gesture, took her hand in a strong grip, leading her upright and looking fully into her eyes.

'It is customary for the incoming prince to lead the dance before supper. Will you join me in my pleasant duty as soon as this ceremony is done?'

'Your request is my command, sir.' Caitlin hoped her response to his magnetic gaze was not evident to the whole room.

'In that case, pray remain at hand, my lady.' He signaled for her to stand to the left of his throne before turning his attention back to the remaining procession.

Recorders, flutes and drums announced a spirited tune as the prince escorted her to the center of the floor, where he guided her in the steps of some dance stored deep in the recesses of her memory. Perhaps she'd seen it in movies? Will was an assertive partner, leading her easily. Soon everyone joined in and the room became a kaleidoscope of brilliant costumes, laughing faces and graceful movement. Caitlin was passed from partner to partner as quadrilles were announced, yet somehow she always ended a pattern drawn to stand facing Will, like two magnetic forces. Dizzy from the energetic dancing and the warm clasp of his hand, she did not know whether to feel regretful or relieved when another fanfare announced the commencement of feasting.

Helpers began to carry laden serving dishes from the kitchen. At Caitlin's table, a splendid array of home-baked bread, soups, vegetables and meats already lined the trestles. Master cooks had excelled in designing ornamental pieces. A magnificent peacock adorned one table, its appearance so realistic it had the look of a stray bird that had invited itself to the feast. A boar's head on a shoulder-high platform was carried in by four men to the accompaniment of hearty singing. Molded like the peacock from some sort of cake base, its tusks were made of parsnips and its ears of flat bread, the whole effect enhanced by shaped marzipan.

Members of the society obviously went to great lengths to reproduce the costumes, food, song, dance, and ceremonies from the history books. Fathers practiced the skills of defense and warfare, mothers saw to food and dress and children absorbed an awareness of their distant ancestors. In the guise of games, elegance and romance could be accommodated in modern life, and Caitlin could only find herself agreeing.

Never a large eater, she nibbled at various dishes. Her emotions were stirred up and all appetite had disappeared. She watched Will who, seated at the head of the main table, quaffed his goblet of mead and sampled quail and pheasant with evident gusto. Ladies seated to his right and left fluttered eyelashes and listened intently to his every word, but Caitlin could not detect any response on his part. He laughed and chatted almost as though they were men and comrades. Perhaps the light flirtation he'd shown toward her was no more than an old-fashioned turn of phrase. He must be unconscious of his own physical magnetism — the quality that drew all eyes toward him. On the other hand, Heather's warning ran through her mind. Will might be an experienced lady-killer whose technique was so polished he needed to exert no effort. Some men thought no more of flirting than of swatting a mosquito. It was an automatic reflex that fed their vanity and left them free to wander on to the next conquest. If so, he was a man to keep at arm's length, as Heather had hinted. The let-downs and hurts of the past year swirled in her chest until her breathing felt constricted. If this man thought she was easily taken in, she was just the girl to educate him.

'Are you feeling okay?' Heather was

concerned. 'You've hardly eaten anything. Have you tried any of the subtleties?' She passed a dish of sweets shaped in individual designs: roses, shells, flat coins.

'They're too exquisite to eat!' Caitlin chose to sample one. 'What's this drink?'

'Mead. A kind of wine, made from honey.'

'It's quite strong.' Already she felt a little giddy.

'I think someone is about to put a proposal to you,' said Heather, as Will approached the table. Caitlin took a hurried gulp from the goblet.

'May I place a request before the lady from the distant land?' His bow was courtly. 'Would you consider a brief meeting with me at the close of these festivities?'

'What, tonight?' Caitlin, flustered, forgot her medieval manners.

'It is the last night of the old year. A time when promises are made and resolutions formed.' Thoroughly absorbed in the nature of their game, his lips quirked as he went on. 'I wonder if we might discuss these mutual decisions and perhaps appreciate the charm of tonight's full moon together?'

So he was nothing but a flirt, and a fast worker at that. Full moon indeed!

She smiled sweetly. 'As a stranger here, what else can I do but welcome your offer to inspect new kingdoms and make new resolutions.'

'Then you'll come?' said Will, surprised out of his courtly phrases.

'Certainly, sire.' She ignored Heather's kick under the trestle. 'I am an expert in full moons, and welcome comparison with any foreign moon you care to show me.'

'Until then. We'll meet yonder at midnight.' Will bowed and swept away.

* * *

Heather clearly disapproved.

'Caitlin, what's the matter with you tonight? You're asking for trouble, going off with Will at midnight.'

'Perhaps he's the one asking for trouble.' She helped herself to a second glass of mead from the tray carried past by a serving woman. 'Don't worry, I'm not about to fall for lines about the full moon.'

'You're being silly. Think about it! Handsome man, warm night, romantic overtures. What makes you think you're different from any other girl?'

'I'm a Scorpio. Our wiles are famous. We don't just drift into one-night stands.'

'But people on holiday often behave out of character . . . ' Heather was genuinely worried about her, but Caitlin smiled and took her hand.

'I know you've always looked after me. Truly, I'm not a little girl now.'

'Sometimes I forget that.' She was seven years older than Caitlin and had been her guardian at times when their invalid mother had needed the regular dialysis her kidney complaint required. And while they recovered from the mourning period following Mrs. Tapper's sudden death, Heather had seen her sister through her last two years of schooling, and encouraged her to follow her chosen career as a nurse. Only when Caitlin was properly launched into adult life would Heather agree with Tony's proposal to shift to Australia. She knew nothing about the painful lessons Caitlin had learned during the course of her unhappy love affair.

'Please stop worrying. I promise I'll be sensible.' The liaison was too intriguing to pass up. If need be she would show her persistent suitor a few tactics of her own.

Speeches and announcements, singing and dancing filled the rest of the evening. Constant invitations to join the circling, clapping couples on the dance floor kept Caitlin on her feet, whirling and side-stepping in bransles and pavanes until she was giddy. She was careful to drink only water after that second glass of mead. She would need a cool head, she knew, to consider any overtures the Prince of Lochac might have in mind. For there was no denying the fizz of anticipation bringing her body awake as midnight was called and voices were raised in the traditional greeting to another brand-new year. People never tired of hoping for prosperity and happiness and she was no different. It was good to be part of a family, and good to think of love returning to her life. A premonition made her shiver as Will's eyes sought hers among the revelers.

Tony was doing the rounds, saying goodbye. Heather looked dubiously at her sister.

'Why not just call it a night and come home now?' She saw she was wasting her time and nodded. 'All right. Just be sensible. I'll leave you a key in the meter-box.'

'Can I help carry the cargo?' Will was offering to help shepherd the drowsy children to the car but Heather shook her head. 'Everything's under control, thanks. Just take good care of my sister.'

Will appeared not to notice her abrupt tone. Smiling at Caitlin, he suggested, 'Shall we go?'

He was wearing ordinary trousers and an open-necked shirt now, somehow looking just as imposing as in the society finery. As he'd promised, a full moon illuminated the night. Canopied trees were blurs against the navy sky and the air vibrated with the rasp of cicadas, their collective voice so loud they seemed to announce some fateful event.

Will held the door of the Porsche open for her. As she stepped inside, she smiled, comparing this subtle scent of luxury with Tony's well-used van, smelling of oil-cans, fish and chip wrappers and cigarette butts.

'Comfy?' Some soft orchestral music began to play as Will turned on the ignition and maneuvered from the tightly-parked yard.

'Where are we going?' In fact, she hardly cared. Seated beside him, gliding smoothly through the night, she felt there was nothing else to want.

'Where would my lady like to go?' There was that teasing note in his voice again.

'The beach.' Why had she said that? The last time she'd made that suggestion, Richard had been horrified. He'd said someone might see them, or he'd get sand on his clothes and be caught out by his wife. If only he'd been honest with her at the beginning! She'd really believed he was in the process of divorcing. That was the story she'd wanted to hear and she'd fallen for it. But what an idiot she'd been. Never again!

'The beach it is. Are you okay, Caitlin?' He seemed to sense her thoughts had drifted to some inaccessible place.

'Of course. I'm sorry. I'm not sure what century or country I'm in, much less where I'm going with you.'

He didn't miss the double meaning. 'Yes. I wonder where we might be going too. Let's find out.'

They drove in silence, and she felt no pressure to make forced conversation. When he lowered the car window and turned off the music, the distant rumble of breakers blended with the low purr of the engine. Her body felt encased in a cocoon, safe and silent. A group of late-night revelers staggered drunkenly along the road, waving and shouting, and Will laughed.

'They'll regret it in the morning!'

'Hangovers? Oh well, they're having fun.'

'Is that your attitude? Have fun and no regrets?'

Why was he making a casual remark personal? 'No. Not really. I have a few regrets.'

'Romantically?' He swung the car onto a downhill slope toward the beach.

'Well, yes. Hasn't everyone?' When he made no reply she decided to change the subject.

'I've made my New Year's resolution.'

'What's that?'

'Let go of the past. Move on.'

'Admirable.'

'Aren't you going to tell me yours?'

He was coming to a stop, and she breathed in the salty air and heard the rhythmic swell of waves. He reached lightly across the seat and dropped a warm hand on her shoulder.

'My Lady Caitlin, you are too serious for the night's proceedings. A beach walk you want, a beach walk you shall have. And I will bring a rug, in case it takes your fancy to lie back and survey the starry heaven.'

'I plan to stay afoot, sire.' She had to laugh at him. If she ended up on her back tonight, she doubted she would be counting stars.

Leaving her shoes in the car, she walked beside Will over spiky grass that led down to a sandy beach. A sense of freedom engulfed her. Time stopped. The past world of rules and duty rosters, regrets and sorrows, disappeared. She was simply a happy young woman, walking beside an attractive man, needing nothing, perfectly content. Their steps fell in unison. His scent, warmth and strength flowed out to her.

'I know what I want to do.' He'd placed a strong arm around her shoulders. 'Will you watch the sun rise with me?'

'That's hours away!' She had a fleeting image of Heather's face if she stayed out all night with Will.

'I have hours to spare. How about you?'

'There's no important engagement I have to keep.' She kept her tone light, concealing the thrill she felt at the prospect of spending the rest of the night with him.

Will spread the blanket in the shelter of dunes, well back from the tide line. As she sat beside him he lay back, staring at the clear midnight sky.

'What do you make of it all?'

'Make of what?'

'Oh, the universe, the planets, fate . . . '

'That question's too hard for me!

Maybe the stars reflect our lives. Before my trip, I consulted an astrologer.'

She waited for him to scoff, but he just said, 'And what happened?'

She remembered the advert. *Understand your nature and make your dreams come true.*

Desperate for anything to help her make sense of the past year, she'd phoned. The astrologer only asked for her date, place and exact time of birth. Fortunately, among her mementoes, Caitlin had the faded hospital card with its scrap of pink ribbon, recording the birth of a little Scorpio girl, twenty-four years before.

'Tell me about it,' Will persisted. He sounded genuinely interested.

'Her name was Mrs. Abselen.' Caitlin thought back to the sunlit desk and the open file with its dozens of symbols, numbers and geometric lines. *I can see you've been through a lonely year. Are you an incurable romantic? A passionate heart beats under that cool exterior.*

The astrologer had had plenty to say

about Caitlin's romantic nature and desires, but she had no intention of sharing those words with Will.

'She was accurate about my personality, and about certain events last year. She actually predicted this trip. Something about Jupiter.'

'And she was right? You hadn't planned to visit your sister?'

'Good heavens, no!' The hospital usually gave preference to married colleagues who wanted time off over the public holidays. 'I expected to spend Christmas working.'

Heather's bank transfer and invitation had come out of nowhere. Lost in a whirl of bookings and packing, Caitlin filled her suitcase with summer clothing, a camera and cosmetics, and tossed in the lucky horoscope. It had delivered a holiday. Perhaps its cryptic symbols had more secrets to reveal.

'Interesting.' Will shifted on the blanket. 'What else did this lady predict?'

And as your fifth house is involved, I

foresee a new love interest in your life.

Caitlin did not answer. She was having trouble ignoring the signals his nearness was stirring up in her body. The slightest contact with him sent delicious thrills coursing down her arms and legs, reminding her how easy it would be to snuggle against him and simply turn off her thoughts. He radiated some unconscious mastery, making her want to trust and follow his decisions. But that contradicted all her sane decisions. She had to be independent. Again, Mrs. Abselen's advice was whispering in her ear. *You can't live in solitary confinement, my dear. You must learn to trust again.*

'I've told you enough. What sign are you?'

'Taurus. That's all I know. I'll never find out the details.'

'Hospital records? Family?'

'I'm adopted.' His tone told her he did not want to talk about it. 'Guess that's why I married so young — looking for a family of my own.'

Her body stiffened. Not another married man!

'What's wrong?' He had felt her involuntary withdrawal. 'I've been divorced for seven years. What would I be doing here with you, if I had a wife at home?'

He could sound as offended as he liked. She would have avoided a lot of heartache if she'd clarified this issue with Richard at the start.

'Some men are devious,' she said flatly.

'You think I'm devious?'

'We're strangers, Will. I don't know anything about you.'

'Likewise. Is that a good reason to think I'm lying to you?'

The full moon he'd playfully offered her at the hall was now high in the heavens, casting its silvery light over the shadowed sea. She could barely make out his features, and his tone of voice was cool.

'I don't think you're lying to me. I believe you. I just needed to be sure.'

'You want to see my divorce papers?'

The teasing note had crept back into his voice. 'I'm sorry, officer, they're at home, I don't carry them with me.'

She laughed, but now he was concerned. 'Someone's hurt you,' he murmured. 'I can understand.'

'How can you?' Of course he couldn't know about Richard's broken promises and lies.

'If it helps, I know what it feels like to be let down by the person you love. You say we're strangers but you don't seem like a stranger to me. I can't explain . . . '

'You don't have to. Let's just enjoy the night.'

The surf breathed its deep, relaxing rhythm, draining her resistance. Whatever warnings Heather had given her, she felt a sense of trust in this man.

'Yes. Let's do that.' Will propped himself on an elbow, cupped her cheek in his hand and placed a gentle kiss on her mouth. A kiss that was a question, or a reassurance. A kiss with no expectation, no demand. A kiss that waited, and would accept whatever she decided.

Confusion rocketed through her body, fighting the ache to respond.

Don't rush into this. It's too soon. Be careful.

But his touch, his masculine aroma, the persuasion of his warm lips, all flared. Pounding heat ran through her body. Relaxing into his arms, she yielded, turning her face up to his possessive lips.

He drew back from their embrace, breathing audibly. Her heart racing, lost in desire, she waited.

'I'm rushing things. I shouldn't keep you out all night. They'll worry.'

Of course he was right. Heather would imagine the worst. There was truth in her words that a holiday mood and a handsome man might sweep away common sense. Caitlin slowly sat up.

'Do you mind, Caitlin? You really are an attractive woman. If we spend the night here, I don't want to take responsibility for the outcome.'

She gave a husky laugh. 'I feel the same.'

'How long will you be staying?'

'Several weeks. I have extra leave due, so my return date's flexible.'

'Excellent! Let me show you around the city. And I'd like to drive you out of town, to the Central Coast.' Springing to his feet, he pulled her upright and hugged her hard, his hands grasping her tiny waist.

'Come on, my Lady Caitlin, before we change our minds.'

Grabbing the rug, he led her down toward the breaking waves. The sand changed to sludge underfoot. Breakers swirled around her ankles and suddenly, laughing, she ran into the shallows, not caring her skirt hem was soaked. Teasingly she called, 'Can't catch me!'

Will followed, swept her up in his arms and carried her along the tide line, zigzagging as though outrunning the build-up of tension they both felt. Slowing, he set her down.

'Let's go home.'

Unexpected words. Somehow, they gave her a feeling of safety and intimacy. One day, perhaps, a trustworthy man would say just that, and she would nod and rest her head against his jacket, hugging him, breathing him in, before they walked side by side, a couple, going home.

She must really want that! Tears had come into her eyes. Lucky it was dark. It would have been hard to explain her sudden yearning to Will.

'Your shoes must feel awful,' she said.

'Not good.' He laughed, and the ache in her chest passed. Her skirt clung unpleasantly to her calves as she climbed shivering into the car.

'Tuck this around you.' He passed her the rug.

Will did not talk and she had nothing to say, though the silence was not uncomfortable. Outside Tony and Heather's house, he leaned across and lightly kissed her.

'Happy New Year.'

'And to you.'

The night had run its course. She waved as the car slid smoothly from the pavement.

There was no key left for her. Eventually she had to knock on the back door and Heather undid the deadlock, staring at her sister's dripping dress.

'I tripped and fell.' It was a half-truth. Her night with Will had been a head-over-heels fall into emotions she'd locked firmly in the basement of her heart.

'Put the dress to soak in cold water. We'll deal with it in the morning.' Heather yawned. 'I'm going back to bed.'

Caitlin settled in the spare room bed. There, the moon directly lit the thin cotton curtains, spotlighting her wakeful form as she lay reliving those magical moments on the beach, wishing Will might be beside her now.

2

Before the family stirred, Caitlin crept into the laundry. The marks on the white dress rinsed away easily, to her relief. Even at this hour the sun's warmth struck her bare arms as she picked her way across the brittle grass and pegged out the dripping muslin gown. What a night! Since arriving here, her life had changed in every way. Kookaburras cackled in the unfamiliar trees, her nieces had grown from toddlers to endearing children, and the numb feeling in her heart melted as she thought of Will. His sensual kisses could so easily have swept away her common sense. He'd taken control and practised restraint, still making it plain how much he wanted her. When would she see him again? Perhaps he would call in or phone today.

In the kitchen, Jackie and Katy were

helping themselves to breakfast. In their shorty pajamas, tendrils of damp hair framing their sleepy faces, they looked adorable and she bent to hug them both. Already she'd missed several years of their childhood. She was their only aunt and they'd hardly remembered her when she arrived. Children did not live in the past; they soon adapted to new places and friends. Would they forget her once she left?

'Are you pleased I'm visiting you? I miss you both, you know.'

Intent on their breakfast, Katy just pointed to the cupboard and Jackie asked, 'Can you reach the cornflakes, Caitlin?'

'Hi!' Yawning and tousled, Tony wandered in and grinned at the sight of Caitlin busy with bowls and milk carton. 'Has the jug boiled?'

He always took Heather a cup of tea in bed before she would face the day. She'd never been a morning person, unlike Caitlin who was wide awake as soon as she opened her eyes.

It must be nice to have a partner who was a friend as well as lover.

'I hear you made a late night of it?'

'I really enjoyed myself. I didn't expect to, but I did.'

'The society's good fun. You went for a midnight swim?'

'Not quite. That was an accident.'

'Swept off your feet by a tsunami?'

'Something like that.'

Swept off her feet . . .

Wanting to be by herself, Caitlin poured the tea and carried her cup back to the bedroom. She needed privacy to process last night's events. The last thing she'd expected or wanted was to meet a man like Will. His face had been the first image in her mind when she awoke and she kept hearing his voice as though he was already in her life, talking to her. Drowsy, she drifted away into a dream, reliving the magic of his kiss.

Cicadas rasped monotonously as another day of sticky heat sapped everyone's energy. Fractious after their late night, the girls grizzled and fought until Heather lathered them with sunscreen, planted sun hats on their heads and sent them off to their above-ground plastic pool.

The glamorous woman who'd curtseyed and smiled last night was gone. In old shorts and stretched T-shirt, she made the beds, cleared the dishes and put on a load of washing. Caitlin worked beside her, helping where she could.

'Did you and Will enjoy yourselves?' Heather lugged the basket of wet washing to the clothesline and began to peg out, her tone casual.

'He was good company.' Caitlin had a wary feeling she was about to be cross-examined and swallowed her own urge to find out more about Will.

'Where did you go?'

'I don't know. A lovely beach. It wasn't far. We just strolled and chatted, you know . . . '

Her voice softened at the romantic memory of that lovely silver moon pouring its light over the dim features of Will as he bent to kiss her.

'You seem to be all in one piece.' Heather's two-edged words were suddenly annoying. If she knew something about Will, she should just come out and say it. What was with all the innuendo?

'Can I help you with anything after we've finished this? If not, I might go and lie down for a while. I just can't get used to this humidity.'

True enough, but Caitlin didn't want to end up saying something she might regret. Heather had been generous enough to make this holiday happen.

'Go ahead. I need to supervise the girls while they're in the pool.'

Caitlin was stretched out in the spare room, an old fan creakily stirring up the humid air, when she heard Tony's crazy mobile ring tone, then his footsteps on the wooden floorboards.

'You awake, Caitlin? Will wants to talk to you.' With a grin he handed her the phone.

'My greetings to the Lady Caitlin.'

Immediately his banter brought an answering response and the morning's tensions disappeared.

'And to you, my lord. I am recovering from our revelries.'

'Are you otherwise engaged? I could escort you to the sights of our fair city.'

'I'd love to!' She hesitated. 'I must check with my family. I'm not sure what they're planning.'

'You ask their leave, and I'll come anyway. If you have a prior claim on your time, I'll only kidnap you briefly. See you within the hour?'

Before she could respond, he was gone. Invigorated, she went to share her plans but Heather sounded offended.

'You're going out? I thought we'd eat by the lake and have a swim.'

It was almost as though Heather had made up her plan merely to make Caitlin change her date.

'We can do that, if you like. We can invite Will to come.'

'No thanks. No. You go. Enjoy

yourself. Never mind about us.'

Caitlin stood indecisively. She couldn't telephone Will since she didn't know his number. Why was Heather being so difficult? They could take a picnic to the lake any time. For some reason she did not want Caitlin to go out with Will. And she wouldn't explain.

Heather's mood mystified her, but it wasn't her problem. She wasn't on duty, obliged to tune in to the needs of her patients and set her own feelings aside.

'Honestly, I'd hate to spoil our holiday. I'd love to go out with you and Tony. I had no idea you'd made plans.'

Surely Heather's mood would soften. She still looked stiff and annoyed.

'Will only suggested a drive. I won't be out long. Can't we go to the lake this afternoon?'

'I suppose.'

There were wails from the pool. Caitlin turned away as her sister shouted at the girls to stop their water fight. Heather had no right to control her like this. Was she having trouble accepting her little sister had grown up and had a life of her own? Maybe she was jealous — stuck at home with two small children while her sister set off on the arm of a handsome man. But she had chosen marriage, she had Tony and, as far as Caitlin could tell, they were happy together. Now it was her turn for happiness.

She changed into a cool white sun frock, applied lip gloss and skin foundation and added a spray of perfume. Her window overlooked the street and, when Will's Porsche pulled up, she went straight out to meet him.

'Ready?' He stepped out and opened the passenger door, his expression telling her he liked what he saw.

She called, 'I'm going now, Heather,' but there was no answer. She must be outside with the girls still. Sinking into the welcome relief of air conditioning, she sighed.

'Bliss! I don't know how people function in this climate.'

'You adapt. This is one of the temperate zones of Australia. You ought to try the Northern Territory sometime!'

'I doubt it.'

Soft music was soothing away the morning's conflict. She sat back, enjoying the novelty of a new city as suburbs spun past. The boat-dotted harbor and arching span of the harbor bridge reminded her of Auckland, but her home town had nothing like the Opera House, crouched there like a powerful white bird preparing for flight.

'Imagine going to a concert there!' She wished she'd brought her camera. 'Was there really so much trouble over the cost and design?'

'The bean-counters thought so. But beautiful things cost what they cost.'

She glanced across as he focused on the traffic. Like an emperor on an ancient coin, Will's profile displayed close-curling black hair, regular features and a solid neck, rising up from a dark, open-necked shirt to support his head with dignified carriage. His casual clothes would undoubtedly carry expensive labels, but she sensed he did not buy quality to impress, but rather because he liked the best and could presumably afford it.

'We're coming to the heart of Sydney now.'

He drove past parks, cathedrals, and shopping arcades fronted by lovely old buildings.

'Enjoying yourself?'

'I love it! Everything's novel.'

'There's plenty more to see. The Rocks, Chinatown, Darling Harbor, the Chinese Gardens . . . '

He was enthusiastic, like a visitor himself. She could detect nothing guarded or contrived in his responses. Heather's insinuations were a mystery.

'Do you know my sister well?' Surely that question would disconcert him, if there was any secret.

'They're a great family. Those cute kids . . . Tony and I get along well. The society's a bit of light relief. I'm working most of the time.'

Nothing there to raise alarm bells. 'What work do you do, Will?'

'This and that.' He waited to allow a car to pull over into his lane and the driver tooted gratefully. 'These days, I renovate properties. Old houses. Warehouse conversions.'

'How did that start out?'

'Doing up my own first home. I discovered I had a knack for retaining the charm while adding the mod cons people want. Originally, I trained as a physiotherapist and remedial masseur. I still keep my hand in, working from home. A few of the sports clubs send me clients. How about you, my lady?'

'I'm a nurse. I do a little massage myself.'

'That doesn't surprise me. Thought you had that look — sympathy and fluffed-up pillows!'

'Are you insulting me?' She laughed.

'Definitely not. I'm all in favor of kindness. There's nothing to recommend chaos.' Just for a moment there was an odd note, almost bitter, in his tone. 'And who do you massage?'

'My patients, if they're in need of some TLC.' Often the residents in the geriatric wing had lost their partner and suffered from the loss of an affectionate touch.

'Would you like to see my place?' He swung left. 'I'd like your opinion on what I plan to do. It's a shambles right now, but I have to live on-site or I lose half the profits in tax.'

Soon they were driving through a coastal suburb where the azure reaches of the Pacific Ocean gathered and surged against the rocky beaches below. Along the cliffs, huge modern mansions and pole houses were interspersed with shabby cottages yet to be bought up by developers looking for prime real estate.

'This area's undergoing a facelift, as you can see.'

He must have a good eye for money, if his car and his apparel were any evidence.

'I suppose everything old will be torn

down and replaced with acres of glass.'

'Not in my case. Here we are. There's a bit of a climb.'

He parked on the steep street and indicated a neglected house standing high among thorny bushes and half-dead native trees. Overgrown nasturtiums straggled around her ankles as she followed him up the precarious steps. She could understand why he'd bought the place, despite its rusted gutters, peeling boards and sagging roof. The view of the ocean was fabulous.

'Careful, the veranda's seen better days. Keep to the planks.'

She took his offered hand, the contact setting off a tingle of electricity. Perhaps he felt it too; he seemed to hold her hand a fraction longer than necessary as she stepped off the improvised foot bridge. Then with a gesture of pride he gazed out at the view. 'What do you think?'

'Amazing. But you have a huge amount of work to do.'

'Keeps me busy. This will be my fifth

renovation. I think I've learned enough to handle it. I've made a start inside. Come on in.'

Entering by the lovely old door with its stained-glass insets, he ushered her into a high-ceilinged hall and indicated an unfurnished room to the right. Leadlights and a window seat drew her gaze to the sash windows that would admit cool ocean breezes. A fireplace of beautifully-grained timber attracted her eye.

'You restored this?' She ran her hands over the silky wood, and Will nodded.

'Tasmanian oak. My pride and joy. The previous owner had painted it khaki.'

He must have a lot of patience. She'd recently stripped and stained a small cupboard at home and knew the amount of work involved.

'I can see you pay attention to detail.' She'd noticed the authentic light pull on its long cord, and the timber-mounted brass switches.

'I've just finished taking up the floor coverings, ready to stain the boards. That will be one of the last jobs, but I couldn't stand the smell of the old carpet. The old woman who owned the place must have run a refuge for stray cats.'

'Oh yes! I can just see the floors polished and set off with Persian rugs.'

'Down the track, yes. You look entranced. The place just overflows with ideas, doesn't it? I visualize a breakfast nook out there, under the grapevine.'

The courtyard was, at present, half-buried in broken furniture and building materials. Will certainly had wide-ranging plans. It must be so rewarding to design modern facilities within the charm of this old retreat.

She was acutely aware he'd come up behind her and was standing close, his mouth a few inches from her ear. 'It's a pity you're only on holiday. We could pool ideas.'

Her heart was throbbing as his hand

skimmed her bare arm. Disconcerted, she stepped away.

'I'm sure you have plenty of ideas of your own.'

'Come and see my massage room. It's the only one that's fully finished.'

She followed him along the passageway, her skin still tingling from that brief contact. Pushing open the door marked 'Clinic', he stood back and she stepped inside.

Dappled cream walls reflected the flickering colors of refracted light as crystals swung suspended from the skylight. Outside the screened window, a breeze stirred ripples of shadowy foliage. The soft sound of bubbling water accompanied brilliant tropical fish circling in a spotless tank. Potted plants sprouted greenery and the room was subtly aromatic with various oils Will used for his treatments. A shelf of CDs and a small sound system completed the sensual atmosphere.

Will noted her approval.

'Caitlin, I'd like to offer you a

massage. Compare notes on the techniques we use?' He sensed her hesitation. 'No funny business! I want you to unwind. You don't seem relaxed. When I called for you this morning, there was a real air of tension. Let me help?'

How tempting! What harm could it do? She could hardly remember the last time she'd permitted herself to stretch out and let trained hands ease away the knots in her shoulders and neck. Richard had never had the slightest idea of non-sexual touch. Somehow the false situation she'd been in with him had distorted everything.

'Here.' He handed her a big towel. 'Wrap this round you. I'll leave you while you change. Make yourself comfy while I put on a CD. The sound's wired through from the front room.'

When he'd gone, Caitlin slipped off her sun frock. Keeping on her briefs and bra, she hitched herself onto the high table and pulled the towel up to her chin. Soft echoes of orchestral music played as she settled back, watching the crystalline flashes as they danced. With a discreet knock, Will entered the room and began to choose from an array of oils and powders.

'Herbs interest me. I think I'll use my orange and neroli blend for you. Opens the heart for joy and happiness, and attracts positive energies. Sounds right for someone on holiday?'

'Sounds fine to me.' She lay on her back, smiling up at him.

'Ready?' He went to work at the end of the table, pressing hard into the sole of her foot.

'Ouch!'

'Tender there? It's associated with the abdominal area. Any bowel problems?'

He glanced up at her peal of laughter. 'Funny?'

'No. Sorry. I'm ticklish.' How could she say she'd been suspicious of his motives? No man with designs on a half-naked female would ask about her daily habits! Relaxing completely, she let her body sink into sensation, realizing just how starved she was for simple touch. She'd been punishing herself over Richard by giving to her elderly patients the gentle care she must have longed to receive herself.

Will's hands were stroking her calf muscles, touching behind her knees and smoothing her thighs. The oil had a delicious moistness and he used it sparingly, so she did not feel greasy. She felt supple fingers work up to the line of her briefs. Now she felt comfortable as he eased the elastic down to her hips and began a circular massage of her stomach.

'A few knots here.'

She often carried stress in that area and had to avoid eating when she was overtired or upset. His deep strokes drew tension out of her until she wanted to sigh out loud. His fingers slid under her ribs to unhook the bra, exposing her small breasts. With more oil, he worked over her chest, again in circles, his palms just brushing her nipples. Her eyes were tightly closed now, denying any intimacy in his professional touch. He seemed to see her body as a whole — nothing more nor less personal. She felt herself sink drowsily into a place of safety and pleasure.

Working down her arms, taking each hand in turn, he interlaced their fingers, pressing into her palms as he had treated her feet. He held each finger, rotating it, and stroked her forearms, elbows and upper arms, taking their weight while she sagged like a rag doll in his grasp. As he caressed her throat and neck she slipped into surrender, vaguely sensing him move to the head of the table to begin work on her face. Her dainty ear lobes were particularly responsive and she suppressed a tiny shudder as he squeezed each one lightly. He pressed her eye sockets, ran his fingers down her small nose, and traced her cheekbones and temples before rubbing her scalp in kneading movements.

'Ready to turn over?'

She felt no resistance as his hands rubbed her back with long gliding strokes. Lightly he massaged the base of her spine, and thrills of physical pleasure shot through her pelvic area. She felt his strong palms press into the wider fleshy areas of her hips and buttocks before he aligned the elastic of her briefs again and moved on to her shoulders.

She was in some halfway world of trust and pleasure when he spoke.

'Nearly done.'

She felt brushing touches up and down her back. He was using his fingertips, and finally the hairs of his arms, to create feather touches of farewell. She felt the light sprinkle of talcum powder on her skin. He rubbed it in gently, and pulled the towel over her relaxed form.

'Don't get up yet. There's no hurry. I'll leave you now.'

She heard the door open, then close.

The music had finished. All she could

hear was the quiet bubbling of the aquarium filter. She lay still, exploring the peace and relaxation infusing her whole body. She was in a vacuum. The past didn't matter. Future plans were non-existent. Everything was here. She noticed how soft the pillow felt against her cheek. Allowing herself to drift, Caitlin fell asleep.

* * *

'Awake?'

Will was standing in the doorway.

'I must have drifted off to sleep.' Caitlin struggled to sit up.

'Hey — you are a nervy girl! No need to get up so quickly. You can feel faint after lying flat for hours.'

'Hours!'

'You had a late night, remember?' He sounded amused. 'Take your time. I've made a late lunch, when you're ready.'

'What time is it? I'm supposed to be going out with Heather and the family.'

'Why not phone her and put her

mind at rest. Use my mobile.'

She tried, but the dial tone rang and rang until she gave up.

'See? They've sensibly gone off to enjoy themselves. That's what you ought to do.'

There was no point in rushing home. Heather might have locked her out.

'Like quiche? I'm afraid we won't be eating in style. The kitchen's 'in original condition', as they say.'

Caitlin stepped onto the brown linoleum flooring of a dingy room with a rusty three-element stove, terrazzo bench and chipped enamel sink.

'This reminds me of the house where I grew up. My mother was never well enough to bother about renovations.'

'She's an invalid?'

'She died when I was sixteen. Heather was still living at home so she took over until she married Tony.'

'And your Dad?'

'He suffered from depression. It wasn't talked about then. Life just got too much for him.'

Her voice made it clear she did not want to go into details and Will did not probe. He indicated the packing case, duly covered with a plastic tablecloth, knives and forks and two unmatched glasses.

'My lady, please be seated on this elegant fruit box while I summon the repast.'

He lifted a delicious-smelling quiche from the microwave. Caitlin helped herself to tossed salad and a big chunk of crusty bread. Her mouth was literally watering for a normal meal.

'Sparkling water? Sorry, I don't keep mead on tap.'

She laughed. 'A little mead goes a long way.'

'As we discovered on the beach?'

If he was implying they'd had too much to drink, she couldn't agree; any more than she could blame the full moon for that most romantic of kisses. She ate in silence until Will pushed the quiche toward her and she cut another slice. She couldn't remember when she'd last enjoyed food so much.

'Do you like being a bachelor?' He must have learned basic skills to whip up a meal like this.

'I enjoy whatever state life places me in.'

She thought that a strange answer. 'There are other options, surely?'

'Once bitten, twice shy. Some women instantly fall in love with my Porsche. How am I to know?'

'That's a bit cynical.'

'That's me!' It was his turn to deflect personal questions. 'Shall I brew coffee?'

'Thank you.'

As Will worked at the bench, she glanced at various postcards, bills and photos secured on the fridge door with magnets. One image was of a beautiful young teenage girl; someone important to him, surely. Curiosity made her ask, 'Who is this?'

'That's Pattie,' he said, as though everybody knew who Pattie was. Again he chose not to explain further. 'What would my lady like to do this afternoon?'

'I'll check whether Heather's back.'

Will handed her his phone. There was still no answer. Very lightly, Will reached over and smoothed the frown lines above her nose.

'You're a conscientious person, aren't you?'

'You don't understand, Will.' She couldn't explain the opinion Heather had of him. She only knew that his touch conveyed concern. He did not seem the kind of man to practice deceit, or pretend to be anything other than himself. Heather's attitude was a mystery.

'What do you say to this? I'll drive you home, but on the way let's take a little walk around town. Most of the shops will be closed, but there's plenty to see.'

'Why not?' It hardly mattered what she did. Heather was bound to misconstrue her actions.

Rapt in the pleasure of a new city

and the company of Will, she lost all track of time as they explored monuments, historic buildings and the huge Darling Harbor complex. Tired as she felt, she wanted to extract every drop from this day, and store it carefully among her most precious memories. Yet she dozed in the car, and was bitterly disappointed when he gently shook her awake.

'You're home, and I'm running late for an appointment.'

'It's been a fabulous day, Will. Thank you!'

'My pleasure, my lady!'

Caitlin waved as he drove away, staring as a boy ran out from the neighboring house and tossed a stone after the Porsche.

'Stop that!' she called, and was rewarded with a rude gesture before the child ran inside. Still half asleep, she stumbled to the open back door and saw the family were already seated around the table, eating dinner. Tony called a cheerful greeting and the girls said hello, but Heather's face reflected cold displeasure. Caitlin was too tired to explain she'd phoned and found no one at home. She walked through to her room, unable to block out Heather's voice as she said, 'Not even a word! She's changed so much I hardly recognize my own sister.'

Tony said something placating but his wife was apparently ready for an argument.

'If I'd known she was like this, I'd never have asked her to come.'

'For heaven's sake! Haven't we had enough dramas lately, Heather?'

A cold silence followed, then the grizzles of children reacting to their parents' argument.

In her hot room, Caitlin opened the window and raised voices echoed from next door. Why was everyone so edgy? Weren't Tony and her sister happy? The stuffy heat brought her out in perspiration and she thought wistfully of that promised swim. Really, living in other people's houses could be trying. Could she have a shower, or was it the girls' bath time? There might even be water restrictions. She didn't know the rules here. Toying with all the possible ways in which she might upset Heather, she almost wished she'd stayed back in Auckland for the holidays, where she could do as she liked and stay in the bath all day if she wanted.

A strangled yelp from next door made her slam down the window and cover her head with a pillow. She must have dozed because when she woke the room was dark and she could hear some television show droning in the background. Tony's cell phone rang and she heard him arranging some get-together for the next day. Ever sociable, he could be inconsiderate at times, making arrangements that took no account of Heather's plans. Perhaps that explained why they were fighting. By the sound of things, their loving relationship had taken quite a downturn. Was love too fragile to survive the rigors of everyday living?

The fair thing to do would be to devote the rest of her holiday to Heather and her family, and forget Will. She'd known the man for a day. She was letting her heart rule her again. Impossible as it was, she was on the verge of falling in love with a complete stranger; one her sister clearly disliked. Was she heading straight back into disaster?

Hot and depressed, Caitlin pushed damp hair from her flushed face and wandered out to make herself a sandwich. It felt an age since she'd eaten Will's food with such pleasure. Her mind torn between choosing to pursue him or concede to her sister, she forced a smile as Tony greeted her, a chunk of cheese and a gherkin in his hands.

'Come to raid the fridge too?' He grinned in his engaging way. He might be casual, but his mood was generally good-humored.

'Yes. Will gave me lunch, but that seems an age ago.'

'Have a good time?'

'Terrific. That's the trouble.'

Tony seemed to understand her meaning. 'Worried about Heather? Look, you two need to have a good talk. There's a reason for her attitude and it's more to do with her than Will.'

He rummaged in the jar of pickled onions and speared one with a fork. 'There's more than one piece of news I think she wants to share, Caitlin. Then you might see her moods aren't your fault.'

'She thinks I don't care about her because I'm not the little sister she left in Auckland.'

'Well, that's obvious.' He sounded approving. 'Take a look in the mirror.'

'Tony, should I trust Will?'

But he would not be drawn into her dilemma. 'Ask him. He's coming over day after tomorrow. There's a tournament soon. We'll bash around in the back yard.'

How could she be rational when her heart was knocking on her ribcage and anticipation raced through her body? She had to sort things out with her sister.

'Is Heather still awake?' She needed to show her love, share the secrets of the past year, and erase the awkward distance.

'No. The heat's really getting to her this year. She went off to bed not long after the girls settled.'

'So you're on your lonesome?'

He smiled. Ruefully, she thought. 'I'll have a beer and finish my midnight feast. Join me?'

'I'm too tired. Thanks. I'll have a quick shower and go to bed.'

Tomorrow she would talk to Heather. Relieved, she let her thoughts drift to the day's memories, and Will's sensitive hands caressing her body.

3

Caitlin stretched and yawned.

She could hear the girls bumping about and Heather telling them to sit up and have breakfast. The impatience had left her voice; she sounded like any mother attending to morning routines. Today would be a good time for them to talk and clear the air. Surely the present tension was due to a misunderstanding.

Will surfaced in her thoughts — a much more inviting reverie. A lot had happened in the short time since meeting him. How could she forget the way they'd danced together, or the night on the beach where passion had stirred? Even the simple things, like sightseeing, and the lunch he'd made for her, were fixed in her memory. There'd been nothing to set off warning bells and remind her how Richard, at first, had seemed so frank and open. Heather's insinuations were the only reason she had to doubt.

Yes, it was high time to sort out the problem.

She quickly dressed in shorts and a blouse and joined the family in the kitchen.

'Sleep well?' Heather made no reference to the previous day, and seemed in a good mood.

Perhaps Tony had said something to her.

'Yes, thanks.' She could hardly say the spare room was hot and the mattress uncomfortable. 'The neighbors were arguing, though.'

Heather nodded. 'I'm pleased they're moving. The girls are picking up some colorful language!'

'What are your plans today?' Caitlin dropped bread in the toaster. 'I thought we might go for a walk, just you and me.'

'Tony can mind the girls.' Heather looked pleased.

'Sorry I was out yesterday.' Caitlin was determined to concede to her sister. 'I should have spent the time with you.'

'Look, don't take any notice of my grumps. It's the heat. And there's something else. You'll be an auntie again in July.'

'That's wonderful! Well, I suppose it is?' Heather didn't seem as excited as she felt herself.

'It's a surprise, that's all.' Heather began stacking dishes on the bench, as though wanting to distract herself. 'Tony and I've been through a rough patch. Oh, you know — mortgage, money pressures, second job. It all creates strain.'

'I thought you looked a bit down.'

Caitlin eyed her sister with sympathy. She'd always been there when Caitlin needed support. For years she'd set aside her own plans to keep a home going and ensure her little sister finished school and began her training as a nurse. Once she married Tony, the babies came quickly. She'd never had an opportunity to simply be a carefree young woman.

'I'm not complaining,' Heather said, as though she was being disloyal. 'It's just . . . I was looking forward to some freedom. Once Katy started school next year, I was going to get a part-time job. You get drab and boring just staying home and talking to kids all day.'

'I'm sure Tony doesn't think you're drab and boring.' Caitlin remembered the admiration in her brother-in-law's eyes as he'd sunk to his knee and bowed at the sight of Heather in her dark red silky dress.

'It's really my fault . . . '

What had brought tears to her sister's eyes? Evidently something very personal was troubling her. Caitlin took control, finishing her toast and pushing back her chair. 'Come on, let's get organized and go. You can tell me all about it while we're out.'

Heather nodded. 'I'll ask Tony to keep an eye on the girls.' She went to collect hats, sun screen and the inevitable bug spray. Another hot day was forecast, and Caitlin was beginning to wonder if it ever rained in summer here. Stopping at a small park where a couple of dogs ran about off-leash and children played on the climbing frame, the sisters sat down in the shade. Heather was quiet, as though she'd opened a topic she'd rather not pursue, but Caitlin persisted.

'I just need to know why you want me to avoid Will.'

'I was afraid of that!'

'Why?'

'I told you, I was feeling drab and unattractive. Perhaps I was holding Tony at arm's length. He was working shifts. Sometimes we hardly seemed to connect for days. Then I put my back out, lifting a heavy garden pot I'd been nagging him to move for weeks.'

The dogs gamboled past, their ears flying and tongues lolling out in a game of pure enjoyment. Heather watched them, her expression wistful.

'The girls would love to get a dog.'

'That wouldn't suit you though, Heather.'

'Well, no — the vet bills and the food . . . '

'And your medical history,' Caitlin gently reminded her. She'd only been ten, and her sister in her teens, when Heather developed allergic eczema and the family spaniel had to be given away.

With a sigh, Heather forced her attention back to the story she was telling.

'Someone in the society told me Will was very good at remedial massage. I booked in and had a course of treatments. He'd just bought a house and opened his studio there. The atmosphere's lovely. He'll probably take you there and show you.'

Caitlin did not mention the massage she'd received by Will's skilled hands. She could guess where Heather's story was leading. Boredom, distance between Tony and herself, fantasy and Will's soothing touch to feed the imagination . . .

'I developed a crush on Will.' Heather's voice was low and guilty. 'It was all my way. He didn't know. He certainly never did anything I could misconstrue. But I was sure he must have guessed how I felt.'

'Did he?' For a moment, Caitlin set aside how she'd been drawn into her affair with Richard. At least she'd been single. Heather was a married woman. What about Tony?

'No. It's easy to mistake Will's manner. He's on good terms with women. Friendly, playful, a listener. It's easy to think he has an interest in you. Have you found that?'

Caitlin nodded. That was certainly true. Heather was describing the same reaction she'd felt too, as she watched the Prince of Lochac charm his female partners.

'He's the same with everyone. But to be honest I don't think he's in the market for a long-term relationship.'

Dread crept over Caitlin.

'Why would he lead girls on if he's not interested?'

'I don't think he leads people on. Not deliberately. Let's face it, he's good-looking, charming, he's a natural Romeo, but I honestly doubt he really connects with women. I have an idea he's never recovered from his marriage break-up.'

'That was seven years ago!'

Heather eyed her astutely. 'So he's told you that? You must be on good terms! Usually he doesn't speak about his ex at all. She was supposed to be a real stunner. And a flirt. Her flirting went too far. I hear he threw her out and filed for divorce in a fit of jealous rage. So the story goes, anyway.'

'They didn't even try to patch it up?'

Heather moved restlessly. The heat was building. The mother called her children and headed from the park.

'It's all hearsay, Caitlin. Who's going to cross-examine Will? Not me!'

'And that's all that happened between you?'

'Of course. My back got better, Tony gave up the night shift and I pulled myself together. Now I'm just embarrassed by the whole thing, and you know why I prefer to avoid Will.'

'Did you tell Tony?'

'Yes. He was hurt. But he believes me, when I say it was just a stupid mistake. He knows I love him.'

'What about the pregnancy? Is he pleased?'

'The pill isn't infallible. We certainly weren't planning on another baby. We're both a bit shocked.'

'But you're okay?'

Heather nodded. 'Yes. We're okay. But I hurt Tony and I'm sorry.' Heather tugged at the petals on a dandelion. 'That's worth remembering, Caitlin. When you hurt someone, you can't take it back.'

Caitlin felt a rush of love for her sister and the burdens she chose to carry. Of course she loved Tony and the girls, but duty came before pleasure. Heather had always tried to do the right thing. Now, more than ever, she deserved a break. But how?

'Can I ask you one more thing about Will before we close the subject?'

Heather shrugged.

'Are you sure Will isn't going out with anyone?'

'He's been out with several girls in the society. I've heard them talk. Perhaps they're like me, smitten when he dons the costumes and assumes that courtly manner. You have to admit it's a turn-on!'

'But there's no one serious?'

'I honestly don't know. Will doesn't confide in me. I do see your point. First I warn you off him, then I admit I've fancied him as well! Not very honest, am I?'

Caitlin was swamped in a wave of love, wishing she could offer the gift of freedom, just for a day. Heather was a caring sister, wife and mother, already expecting another child. Hearing her confession somehow made Caitlin want to be equally frank. She decided to keep nothing back about Richard. He'd returned to his wife and family, and she was over the pain of her affair. Yes, she'd been foolish to let it happen. She'd been wrong. Yet the experience was in the past and she'd learned a valuable lesson.

Heather listened without judgment. 'My poor little sister,' was all she said when Caitlin fell silent, tears quivering on her long eyelashes as she recounted the story. 'I guess that's life. We stumble and pick ourselves up. We've both made mistakes. Yet here we are!'

She indicated the beautiful surroundings. 'But we'd better get going. I have a ton of things to do today.'

Despite the heat she walked purposefully, already lost in planning the rest of her day's duties. Council workers labored, mending potholes, and a postman buzzed past on a motorcycle. How did people manage to work in this humidity? The remorseless heat of summer brought Caitlin out in perspiration. All she wanted to do was stand under a cold shower or submerge in the ocean. She tried to imagine being pregnant. Could she ever adapt to such responsibility? Fortunately the new arrival would be a winter baby. The gulf between Heather's life and her own was vast. Marriage, children . . . Would she ever have the resilience to take that step? What sort of man could persuade her to do so? The image of Will came to her as he served her food on a makeshift table. Being with him had felt so natural.

'What are you smiling at?' Heather was waiting at the gate for her to catch up.

Next door, a skinny black dog fled from a rough-looking woman wielding a broom. Caitlin's happy expression faded, though Heather seemed used to her neighbor.

'When are you moving, Val?' she called.

The woman paused. 'Sooner the better. Can't stand this dump. Or that mongrel. He'll catch it, ripped the washing off the line. Come here, you!'

The dog slunk toward her, ears flat and tail drooping. Val raised the broom.

'Come on in for a cuppa,' Heather offered, smoothly diverting the inevitable.

Taking its chance, the dog dashed past and crawled under the house while Val trailed inside, complaining about the kids, the hubby and the heat.

* * *

Yesterday had sorted out their differences, and Caitlin woke determined to stop indulging in thoughts of Will. Nothing could interfere with the rest of her stay. Knowing her sister was pregnant and possibly feeling unwell, perhaps she could cook a few meals. At least she could take Jackie and Katy to the shops or the beach, and give Heather and Tony some space.

She ate a light breakfast, cleared the plates and began to do the washing-up when she felt a light touch on her shoulder. Her skin pricked with recognition. Will was smiling at her.

'Surprised? The front door was open. I came straight in.' He dropped his kit bag and kissed her cheek lightly. 'I see you look good in the mornings, too. Some people take hours to come round.'

How many other girls had he inspected first thing in the morning?

'You'd be an expert?' She sounded sharper than she'd meant and he looked puzzled.

'Expert in what?'

Caitlin moved away. Illogically, perhaps, Heather's confession made her feel she should avoid any sign of intimacy. Will picked up a tea-towel.

'Want a hand?'

'Princes don't wash dishes!'

'Nor do ladies of my court.'

She felt anything but a lady as she stood there in shorts and halter top.

'I guess you're looking for Tony?' It was too hard, maintaining a façade of distance when all she wanted was to hug him and raise her mouth to his lips.

'No hurry. I wanted to talk to you about that drive to the country. I'm making a business trip to the Central Coast in the next few days. May I turn it into a pleasure trip, if my lady will accompany me?'

He couldn't help it. Charm came as naturally to him as breathing.

Caitlin reminded herself impulsive agreements were off-limits now.

'I'd like that. But I have to see if it fits in with other things.'

'Other things?'

He sounded possessive, as though she had to account for her movements.

'My sister was kind enough to pay for my holiday, Will. It's natural we want to spend time together.' Her tone was cool. Surely he didn't think she had a string of other men at her beck and call, all begging her to go on dates? She'd only arrived a week ago!

His expression relaxed. 'Of course. Do try and come, if you can. I'd really like that.'

Did he think she needed persuading? Already, sticking to her resolution was proving difficult.

Tony bounded in. He never seemed to walk into a room like other people. There were usually distant crashes, slamming gates, banging doors, loud and cheerful hellos, long before Tony himself arrived. His exuberance could be wearing, but people usually found themselves smiling and feeling the day had taken a turn for the better whenever he showed his face.

He clapped Will on the shoulder and began to gather up bits of armor lying around on the kitchen floor.

'It's fencing practice first?' Will picked up his kit. 'I'll go and put on my gear.'

'I'll be ready in two ticks.' Tony groaned as a piece of metal dropped on his toe. 'What a business it must have been, trotting off to work in those days.'

Caitlin had a vision of Tony rushing along a cobbled roadway, bits of breastplate scattering to right and left as an indignant horse tried to take flight from its noisy rider. Her peal of laughter drew curious glances from both men as they went to change and headed out to the back yard. Jackie and Katy followed them, carrying beach spades and equipped to do a little fencing of their own.

The kitchen was clear. Caitlin heard the bathroom door close, and after a few minutes Heather wandered in, still in shorty pajamas and looking wan.

'Aren't you well? Can I do anything?'

Heather flopped down on a kitchen chair. 'Tea and an arrowroot biscuit's all I can face.'

'How long does morning sickness last?' The whole business of pregnancy and labor sounded unpleasant. Heather noticed her sister's distaste.

'Believe me, when you hold that little bundle of joy in your arms and look into its eyes, you forget everything you've moaned about.'

'I won't be holding any little bundles of joy any time soon.'

She sounded so determined that Heather laughed.

'What makes you so sure? You just haven't met the right man, Caitlin. When you do, you'll feel different.'

'I doubt it.' But the image of Will appeared unbidden, and she remembered the pounding of her heart as they lay together on the sand. Surrender. Could she ever trust any man enough to explore just what that word meant? She stood staring out the window while Heather went to dress. The men's rehearsal might only be a game, but in their protective headgear they looked inaccessible and somehow dangerous. For twenty minutes they worked through a series of formal moves as each attacked or stepped back, feinting or executing lunges that provoked the other to parry or withdraw.

'They take it seriously,' Caitlin said, when Heather returned. She hadn't been able to take her eyes off the incongruous sight of two grown men acting like this in a suburban back yard.

Will had a natural grace. His moves were lithe and controlled as he side-stepped, jumped or moved forward for an attack that set Tony retreating behind the shield he held in his left hand. Tony's style was pugnacious, rather like a bulldog determined to defend a bone. On the sidelines, the girls followed suit with their plastic spades until the inevitable accident brought Katy howling to her mother for comfort. The men welcomed an excuse to break, pulling their masks from perspiring faces and gratefully accepting cold drinks.

Will voiced his invitation. 'I've asked the Lady Caitlin to accompany me to the country. However, she is determined your claim takes precedence. I therefore request permission to escort her.'

Caitlin was relieved as general laughter followed. A whole day together — such an exciting prospect!

'Wake up, dreamer!'

Drifting in romantic fantasy, she'd

evidently missed Tony's remark. She had to be careful. Will was no prince. His charm could be no more than play-acting, like the convincing way he'd thrust his sword as though fully intending to run it through Tony's heart. He carried off the illusion of his role so well.

'We have an announcement.' Tony took his wife's hand. 'We have another baby on the way.'

Caitlin cast a quick glance at Will, gauging his reaction. She'd gathered he liked children, judging by the easy way he and the girls interacted. He spoke to them as small adults, with no hint of talking down in his manner. Now he sounded delighted, congratulating Heather with a friendly hug. Plainly he saw her only as his friend's partner and mother to their children.

'Intermission's over.' Tony stood up. 'Swords to the ready.'

They resumed their practice while Heather and Caitlin made beds, sorted laundry and prepared a salad for lunch.

'Thanks for helping.' Heather sank onto the couch, fanning her face with a brochure from the hardware store. Her work seemed to go on endlessly. The next time they went out, Caitlin resolved to take over the care of her nieces and allow her sister time to relax.

Will declined an invitation to stay for lunch. He had some other business out of town, and said he would be away for several days. As Caitlin walked out to the car with him, his blue gaze fixed on her as though recording a precious memory. 'No excuses, my lady. On my return, our visit to the far kingdom is secured.'

'That will be my pleasure, sir.'

A game. Only a game. But claiming the heat as her excuse to rest, she retired to the privacy of her room, where she could dwell on the astonishing fact that a week ago she'd never heard of Will Bradshaw. This stranger was rapidly changing her life, overruling her caution, luring her to forget her hard-won resolve. She'd thought independence, work and home would be enough to satisfy her. Now she knew differently. Returning alone to New Zealand held no appeal at all. Impulsive and unplanned as the idea might be, she desperately wanted Will in her life. He'd restored her self-esteem. She was starting to believe in love again.

With Will out of town, at least she could concentrate on her sister and the family. Tony suggested a day out at a local wildlife sanctuary. The indispensable equipment for Australian picnics seemed to be an Esky packed with ice, paper plates and plastic cups, soft drinks, and the inevitable bottle of BBQ sauce. The family found a table near one of the public barbecues, where Heather set out the homemade salads, a cooked chicken, buns and a tray of meat.

Caitlin watched, hiding her surprise as families unpacked portable tables and folding chairs, beach umbrellas, radios, bikes and balls for the children, blankets, towels, cushions, wine glasses and cardboard casks. To her, a picnic was a few sandwiches and a flask of coffee. Here, the outdoors was a second home. Sulfur-crested cockatoos, pink-winged galahs and kookaburras added their various calls to the din. In spacious netted enclosures wallabies and kangaroos shuffled on long back feet to a shadier retreat. Emus inspected the visitors, arching snake-like necks and peering like short-sighted snoopers at the strangers. An arrow indicated the koala reserve, somewhere along a bush track. After lunch she would take the girls for a walk and give Tony and Heather some space.

A sociable cockatoo attracted Jackie and Katy. Delighted to have an audience, it was showing off: running along the branches of its enclosure, swinging upside down, tipping its head sideways and chattering 'How's your mother, Fred?' while the girls giggled and reached up, trying to stroke its feathers.

'Mind your fingers. Those birds bite!' Heather was never off-duty, and Tony began to fire up one of the barbecues. Caitlin settled on the rug, thinking of Will. He was out of the city, who knew where, yet all she could think of was his massage and that kiss she would never forget. She felt connected to him by a psychic link — he could reach out and summon her, however far away he might be. When had she let him invade her heart? This was happening too quickly. Heather had warned her against a short-lived holiday romance. But for now her sister was minding her own business about Will Bradshaw.

The aroma of cooking sausages and steak began to drift over. Heather's morning sickness had settled and she shared a relaxed smile with Caitlin.

'Hungry?'

Caitlin nodded. 'It's perfect here,' she said. For now the negativity of the past had simply been erased. She was with those she loved, and an expansive feeling swept away every worry.

'Grub's up!'

Soon they were eating in silent contentment, broken only by the small disasters that seemed to accompany small children and plates of food, wherever they were. Katy's sausage, dusty and grass-covered, attracted a sharp-eyed magpie who strutted off with his prize as though he'd struck the lottery.

'Chicken?' Heather opened a container of cold sliced meat but Caitlin declined. Her small appetite had yet to catch up with the others, who ate generously, waving their hands like royalty as they warded off persistent little bush flies.

Lunch over, Caitlin offered to take her nieces along the marked bush tracks leading to various animal enclosures. The park was designed with space and natural habitat in mind. A reptile sanctuary housed snakes gracefully twined around branches or curled asleep in leafy retreats. There were no snakes in New Zealand and she had not grown up with the fear most Australians were taught as children. Behind glass, the creatures were harmless and she admired their sinuous lines.

Further along the path a vast netted area housed ducks, budgies, swans and brilliant-hued parrots. Peacocks roamed free and lordly on the grass, one producing a display so magnificent the girls stared, amazed.

'What's he doing?' Jackie said.

'I think he's dressing up to impress his girlfriend.'

'Is he going to get married, like you and Will?'

Caitlin laughed. 'Will and I hardly know each other.' Children were so astute at picking up the secret moods of adults.

'But you want to marry him, don't you?' Jackie eyed the peacock as though she wouldn't mind marrying him herself.

When the animal and bird enclosures had been inspected, Caitlin took a roundabout track back to the picnic area. Tony and Heather had presumably gone for a walk, no doubt pleased to have time alone. And precious time with her nieces would be all too short. She would go home, Heather's new baby would be born, and the most she would share would be some photographs. A return visit would be at the top of her resolutions.

After the breeze and shade of the park, the locked house was unpleasantly stuffy. No wonder Australians had devised an outdoor way of life in summer. The girls argued and grizzled until Heather lost patience and gave them both a light slap, at which they went howling to Tony for comfort. Caitlin kept hoping Will would phone. Now there was a kind of empty space in her day and the feeling displeased her. Dwelling on Will was stupid. She hardly knew him, he had made no promises, and soon she would be leaving Australia.

'I'm not looking forward to going home,' she told Heather.

Perhaps she was angling for a similar sentiment from her sister, who merely said, 'But that's weeks away,' as though it hardly mattered. She had lost her air of relaxation.

'Aren't you feeling well?'

'A bit off-color. It's normal in the early stages.'

'Go and lie down. I'll mind the girls.'

Tony saw she was available. 'I have to pick up a few things at the shops. Okay?'

'No problem.'

Caitlin walked out to the yard, preparing to ask the girls what they would like to do. As Tony's van pulled away, the house phone rang. Caitlin ran to answer it. She felt sure it was Will. But it was a woman, who spoke abruptly.

'Are you Heather's sister? The one from New Zealand?'

'That's right,' Caitlin said, surprised.

'I've just come back from Queensland. I've heard you've been seeing Will.'

'Who are you?' Caitlin was swept by an unpleasant tide of emotion as the nasal voice continued with determination.

'I'm Will's fiancée, that's who.'

'I don't know what you're talking about.'

'Just ask him who Angela is.'

Suddenly the line was dead. Caitlin stood still, color draining from her face and a sick feeling starting to churn in her stomach. Replacing the receiver, she went to the bathroom and splashed cold water on her face as though it might wash away the shock of the caller's words.

Will had never spoken of anyone called Angela — certainly not of a fiancée. Yet why would anyone make such a claim if it wasn't true? Had he been wooing her, charming her, just to win her into some quick holiday affair? Maybe this trip he'd planned was just an excuse to enjoy a fling. Some corny device, like a mechanical breakdown near some secluded pub with only the bridal suite available? Her mind racing, she felt herself shake with anger and disappointment. He was another Richard and not to be trusted. She wasn't a puppet to have her strings pulled by Will Bradshaw. She would pull a few strings of her own. Let him so much as give her a single reason to verify her doubts and he would be sorry they were ever introduced.

4

Caitlin spent the next few days acting as nurse and housekeeper as, one by one, the family members came down with a stomach bug. Heather was the first to discover her upset digestion had nothing to do with pregnancy, and Tony was soon afflicted with similar nausea. Caitlin made a light meal for the girls but they too seemed out-of-sorts and by bedtime were in the same condition as their parents. Caitlin was the only one to escape, but she hadn't eaten any of the picnic chicken, so they decided that was the probable source of their problems. There was little to be done except distract the children and prevent them from pestering their parents, who lay pale and miserable, feeling sorry for themselves as they made trip after trip to the bathroom. Fortunately these illnesses usually passed as quickly as they arrived.

She was glad to take her mind off Will. Whenever she thought of him, unpleasant emotions surfaced. She wished she'd never gone with him on New Year's Eve. She'd walked head first into a complex web of emotion. Now she felt helplessly caught. She was determined to focus on the practical needs of the family, yet as she went quietly from room to room, sponging Jackie's flushed face or changing Katy's pajamas, Will's strong, beguiling image kept appearing in her mind. While she pegged out laundry and carried boiled water in to Tony and Heather, his casual words replayed in her thoughts like a recording.

No one else noticed her state. They were all absorbed in their temporary misery. But by the following afternoon the symptoms were easing and the household was returning to normal. The planned outing with Will now felt like an obstacle. Caitlin rehearsed what she would say and do, sometimes feeling angry enough to plot spiteful paybacks, sometimes simply feeling miserable and disappointed at Will's deceit and her own gullibility. How stupid, trusting another man with her heart! Better to toughen up and develop a cynical attitude toward men. She'd met some women like that among her co-workers — nurses with bitter tales to recount and set expressions warning men away. She'd felt sorry for those soured women who'd settled for self-support and one another's company. They'd laughed when Caitlin said she believed in romance. It was a daydream, they said; something that existed in books and movies. Caitlin was beginning to wonder if they were right.

The evening before their date, Will telephoned.

'I got back last night. Trip was good. I've been up on the roof most of today, replacing iron. What have you been doing?'

He sounded relaxed but Caitlin had no idea what to say to him. The only words on the tip of her tongue were *Who's Angela*? Her heart was racing in that apprehensive way she always felt before a dental treatment. She explained the family illness briefly.

Will commiserated. 'I hope our drive's still on? I'm looking forward to seeing you.'

'Yes,' was all she managed to say.

His cheerful tone changed. 'You don't sound yourself. You haven't got the same bug, I hope? My lady hasn't forgotten our tryst?'

His manner merely annoyed her. He sounded superficial, resorting to a line he fed all the girls.

'I haven't forgotten.'

Her cold tone must have registered. There was a question in his voice. 'You don't sound keen to go.'

'I'm sure the scenery will be lovely.' Her mouth was dry. Her heart thumped, knocking on her rib cage.

'Seven o'clock then. Not too early?'

Now he was brisk and businesslike.

'Seven's fine.'

An awkward pause. If only she had the willpower to hang up and be done with him! She was trembling now. Maybe she did have a touch of the bug. There was no reason to care about Will Bradshaw. She hardly knew the man.

'Perhaps I'd better let you go.' He sounded disappointed, as though she owed him warmth. Well she didn't. She owed him exactly nothing. And unless he had a convincing explanation for Angela's bizarre phone call that was exactly what he would get from her.

She slept restlessly. When she woke at dawn the heat seemed even sultrier, for the room faced the street and overnight the window had to be locked for security. She flung it open and the neglected next-door dog, kept on a short rope in the dirty yard, whined hopefully. Not a good start to the day. She tried to focus on the radiance of the red-streaked sky. The possibility of rain was a pleasant thought, for lawns and gardens were crackly dry and the threat of bush fires real.

She stared at her limited array of clothes. Casual dress was acceptable almost everywhere. Besides, why would she want to impress Will? After today she might never see him again. She settled for jeans, shirt and sandals. With a touch of makeup she was ready. She was too nervous to eat breakfast, and paced quietly, watching the street and waiting apprehensively as she saw Will pull up and walk toward the house.

He knocked quietly and she answered the door. How crisp and groomed he looked, in a white open-necked shirt and dark trousers, his throat and arms tanned golden from outdoor work.

'You look nice.' The words had slipped past her guarded tongue.

Will smiled at her. 'So do you. All set? There's a property I want to inspect. After that, I'm at your disposal. I thought we'd take a scenic drive and stop off at a little place I know for lunch.'

'I'll get my bag,' was all she said.

* * *

Will followed a route she'd taken with him before. Briefly she recognized a few landmarks before he headed toward the harbor tunnel and took an exit route from the city.

'Temperature's set a bit low.' He adjusted the air conditioning and she wanted to run her fingers along the dark curly hairs on his muscular forearm. She sat primly, her hands folded in her lap.

'Would you like music?'

'If you like.' Anything to fill the need to make conversation . . . It was impossible to be natural with him with Angela's claim spinning in her brain. As soon as a suitable opportunity arose, she would clear up that issue, even if it meant catching a train back to Sydney by herself.

He'd noted her stiff manner. For several minutes he pointed out scenic attractions or chatted as they drove, but her mistrust was affecting him too.

Finally he turned up the music; the same CD he'd chosen on their previous outings. She would never hear it again without remembering this brief encounter. The soundtrack tugged so strongly at her emotions she could not bear it.

'Would you turn the volume down?'

His nod was curt. He must think she didn't set much store by their first meetings.

'What's your business project about?' she asked, struggling to seem normal. She couldn't demand an explanation when he was motoring along the freeway.

'Acreage that would suit a block of retirement units. Older people seem to like the area. It's accessible to Sydney, but away from the city rush. My present renovation isn't finished but I like to plan ahead.'

Normally she'd have a dozen questions to ask him. He was explaining something now about the difficulties of engineering the main road through the rocky landscape, while she stared out the window. The wide highway carried them above the Hawkesbury River. On its banks were jetties and holiday houses, and she drifted into romantic fantasy, where one of the cottages belonged to her and Will. The smooth ride lulled her as she let her head rest back, just a hand's breadth from his powerful shoulder. He reached for his iPod and plugged in earphones, effectively cutting himself off from communication. She fell into miserable self-pity, imagining him with Angela, Heather, Pattie (whoever she was) and his ex-wife.

Unexpectedly, he wrenched the car onto a turn-off. After several minutes he parked under trees where summer heat had not yet sapped the green from the long sweet grass.

'Are you going to tell me what's going on?' He was staring straight ahead, his profile unsmiling. 'You obviously regret coming with me today, but I must say I'm completely in the dark as to why.'

He wasn't a man to avoid confrontation. She would only have to say the word and he would take her straight to the nearest transport back to Sydney. There would be no begging or pleading, the way Richard had behaved when she'd ended their relationship. She had to speak up or lose him, and live with the everlasting doubt she'd thrown away a precious chance for happiness.

'I had a phone call the other day, from a girl called Angela.' He showed no reaction. She went on, with a hint of anger. 'Apparently your fiancée. She told me to ask you.'

Will ran his fingers through his thick hair. He looked astonished.

'Do you mean Angela from the society?'

'I have no idea. Are there several?' Her coldness masked her deepest fears, now surging through her, clenching her hands and settling in a hard knot in her throat.

He didn't seem to notice how close

she was to breaking down.

'I don't know any others.' He sounded bemused. 'There's one Angela in our group — you remember, where we met?'

'Of course I remember!' She was ready to snap. Did he really think she cared so little?

'We did go out on group outings, a few times. And when I was to become the new prince, I had to choose a partner as my princess. They usually have simultaneous crownings. I thought Angela would play the part well. She's a born actress, belongs to an amateur theatre group.'

Caitlin was starting to piece together Will's story. But he went on, like a man providing an alibi for some unknown crime.

'Angela began playing her role and the rest of the group joined in. They gave us congratulations and asked about the royal betrothal. It was all in fun. A game! Surely she couldn't have taken it seriously. I hardly know the girl.'

'She took it quite seriously.' It wasn't hard to understand. A romantic girl could weave a fantasy around the handsome Prince of Lochac and his proposal, particularly when the whole gathering joined in the flight of fancy.

'Is that why you were so upset?'

She knew he'd been truthful. She owed him the same. 'Will, we've only known each other a short time. I can't get you out of my mind. It's crazy. I don't know what's happening to me.'

He grinned. 'You've rocked my socks off too.'

She'd never heard such an earthy description of desire before and couldn't help laughing a little, even as she nestled into his strong embrace. The horrible doubts were gone. She rested her hand on his chest, where his heart throbbed hard under her caress.

All her resistance melted. He stepped from the car, gathered a blanket from the back seat and opened her door. In the quiet glade, where invisible birds sang and the springy grass released its sweet crushed scent, he took her hand and lay down with her. Drawing her into a long kiss, he began to trace the contours of her hips and slender waist, stroking her with fingers that seemed to memorize her form. Caitlin closed her eyes, exploring the defined muscles of his back and shoulders with a loving touch. Slowly Will undid her blouse and began to drop light kisses above the fabric of her low-cut bra. He wanted more. He undid the hooks and exposed her small breasts to the open air as his lips moved lower, his tongue circling her nipples. He pressed hard against her, telling her he was ready to make love.

Languor invited her to forget everything but the thrilling sensations lapping through her body. Forcing her eyes open, she saw his features wore a mask of similar sensuality.

'Will. Not here.' Her voice was husky. They were in full view of anyone out for a walk. He nodded and rolled away while she fixed her bra and buttoned her blouse, her fingers trembling from the passion he'd aroused in her.

'You're an odd one.' He shook his head but his tone was affectionate as he dropped a light kiss on her cheek. 'I don't think you know what you want.'

Considering she'd spoiled the day with her silence and accusations, he sounded remarkably tolerant of her mixed signals. Easing her worry, he whispered, 'You know it's only a matter of time, my lady?' and she nodded.

'Yes. I know.'

Her reply satisfied him. He stood up and brushed down his clothing. Caitlin followed suit. He made their future sound so inevitable she felt a glow of happiness.

'Let's get the business side done with, then the rest of the day's ours. I reckon there's rain coming.'

She'd hardly registered how overcast the day had suddenly become. What did it matter? Let it rain, hail, thunder. She was with the man she loved. Forcing down the thought that she had to leave in a few weeks, she settled beside him as he set his GPS for the inspection site and turned the car. Back on the road, he reached over and rested a hand on her thigh.

She wondered why she found it so hard to be direct. Perhaps it was why Richard had been so surprised when she finally talked of the loneliness, jealousy and guilt she'd felt. She was with an honest man now. From now on, she would keep no secrets; dare to trust.

The car skimmed past a landscape of gold, olive-green and dusty brown tones. She was used to the Irish-green hills and valleys around Auckland, where the rainfall and temperate climate never reduced grassland to this thirsty pelt.

'I hope it does rain soon.'

'Why?'

'The land's parched.' She cared for growing things, and liked his enthusiasm as he responded.

'Once I've secured a permanent income,

I plan to leave the city and acquire a small farm. Maybe commercial flower production, or pedigree breeding.'

'You mean bulls? Stallions?'

He laughed aloud. 'No, I'm a dog man. I was thinking German Shepherds, Labradors. They make such great service dogs.'

'I've had a few patients who relied on assistance dogs. They do make a huge difference to people's lives.'

'The idea appeals to you?'

'I've never thought about a change of career. But it does sound like a great life.'

'Mm.' He said no more.

As the car took a turn-off, overhead boughs intertwined to form a leafy tunnel. Shade enclosed them in a private world, so sharply lovely she felt tears come to her eyes. Her emotions were on high, and she felt uplifted from the everyday world. She hadn't meant to fall in love, but it had happened and there wasn't a thing she could do about it.

Will parked outside a padlocked gate. 'This is it.'

'Are you meeting the owner?'

'No one lives here. The agent says there's an old cottage, in need of TLC.' He laughed. 'That phrase is a dead giveaway.'

Climbing over the rickety gate, they walked hand in hand through waist-high weeds toward a house covered in wisteria and climbing roses suffering from the drought. While Will paced out the dimensions of the building project he had in mind, Caitlin walked around the derelict building, peering in grimy windows. She could tell by the remains of the garden that a loving hand had once built this oasis as a reminder of England. There would have been an herb plot and bricked pathways leading to an orchard. Now the earth was infested with weeds and the trees were so unpruned and old they bore no fruit. Her imagination took flight. She'd always dreamed of buying a country retreat to refurbish. A project like that would take years to complete, but she would be in no hurry.

Will picked up on her enthusiasm. He retraced her discoveries, pointing out structural deficiencies. 'The piers need re-blocking and the roof's had it. The place needs a lot of work.'

'It would be a shame to demolish it.' She half-expected him to disagree. His interest was commercial, after all. She realized she would never know the fate of the little house. In a few weeks, she would be on the opposite side of the Tasman Sea.

But the cottage at least was something solid and real. 'If I had the money, I'd be tempted to buy the place myself.'

'What, you'd rebuild, paint, replace the water tank, the sash cords, that crumbling chimney?'

'Definitely. I'd prune and feed those poor old trees and cut back those vines.'

'You're really taken with it!'

Foolishly, she was transferring all her longing for Will, her family and dreams of love onto this tumbledown shack. Resolutely swallowing her sadness, she tried to ask intelligent questions about his development plan. He sounded non-committal. Perhaps the site was too isolated. There'd been no sign of shops or buses. It was simply a haven belonging to a world untouched by pollution, overcrowding and all the rest of the modern problems. She hoped somebody might see its potential as a weekend retreat. More likely, the bulldozers would wipe out all traces of its history forever.

In tune with her negative thoughts, heavy drops struck through her thin blouse and a deafening roll of thunder startled her. She was about to make a dash for the Porsche, but Will grasped her hand as they ran to shelter under the veranda canopy which, despite large patches of rust, retained a few solid sheets of iron.

'Wouldn't we be better in the car?'

'Not in an electrical storm, my love. Lightning can strike a vehicle. That's okay as long as the windows are wound up, but it's rather alarming.'

'We don't have storms like this back home.' She'd seen forked lightning stab the sky and strike a power transformer outside Tony's house.

'I remember being struck once, in a car. The body lit up, there was a bang and the whole vehicle shifted. We're better off here.'

Resigned, they settled on the wooden boards, and Will pulled her against him while the sky flickered with a bluish light and another crash of thunder echoed on and on. She rested her head on his firm shoulder, feeling safe and protected. If this man asked her to give up her modest accommodation and secure job, would she follow him or cling to what she knew? In this country of extremes, was it so far-fetched to imagine such a radical change of course?

She'd formed scattered impressions about Will and she liked the traits he'd shown so far. He was considerate, self-controlled, and a hard worker. The society allowed him to show a more playful side and she thought he liked being chosen for the powerful role of prince. Will knew what he wanted and where he was going. He was no go-getter, but he was decisive. She would have to know her own mind, and be ready to give him an answer, if he raised the subject of their future. She could daydream, sitting here with him in a bubble of time. But perhaps he had no intention beyond enjoying a couple more weeks in her company, then waving a friendly goodbye.

She had to find out more about him.

'You must have been a very young bridegroom?' She needed him to be frank. The rumor that he still loved his ex-wife was bothering her. If he talked about her, surely she would discover his attitude. Besides, she longed to be open with him, too. She did not want any secrets between them. How wonderful to trust a man with the truth, including the mistakes you made through inexperience.

'I was eighteen.'

'Why would you want to get married at eighteen?'

'She was a beautiful girl, my wife.'

So, it had been a physical attraction. Strange he'd used those words. *My wife*. That title should be cancelled by divorce.

'What was her name?' she persisted.

'Her name's Patricia. We were married for ten years. We've been divorced for seven. That makes me thirty-five years old. Any more questions?'

His sarcastic tone surprised her. He'd never sounded so cold before. Heather must be right. Will didn't sound as though he'd moved on from that scar, even now. She ought to drop the subject, yet she wanted to tell him about Richard, and explain why those lingering hurts had made her so edgy at times. On the verge of disclosing her own past, she tried forcing him to tell her why he remained attached to a past love.

'Do you ever have contact with Patricia now?' Deliberately she used the name he did not want to hear.

He grew even more withdrawn. 'As rarely as possible. She lives in Melbourne.'

So he did still maintain contact. 'Has she remarried yet?'

'Not as far as I know.'

Caitlin was tired of her evasive approach. 'Will,' she persisted. 'I know I'm probing. Do you still care for her?'

Her words released a torrent of passionate words that amazed her.

'Care for her? I hate the woman! She was a slut. One man wasn't enough for Patricia. Anybody who fell for her looks and offered her a word of flattery had free entertainment.'

His brooding rage alarmed her. Even if he was speaking the truth, he should have let go of the past by now. And she thought he was exaggerating. His young wife may have been vain, silly, immature, but many girls were susceptible to admiration. Confronted by a hurt, possessive partner, they might well be driven to secretive affairs, feeding their need for reassurance. He'd probably built her up in his memory as far worse than she really was. He needed to bring out whatever he was trying to suppress. Otherwise Patricia's image would go on haunting him forever. If so, how would he ever find the trust to love again?

As she was trying to go further along the delicate path she was treading, he began to speak again. 'I respect marriage, Caitlin. To me it's a sacred institution. Maybe it's because I'm adopted and had to come to terms with not knowing my natural parents. My aunt raised me. She's a sweet old soul but I never felt I belonged.'

His words chilled her. Inside the handsome Prince of Lochac was a small boy, grieving because he felt unwanted.

Will went on. 'I always determined when I got married it would be for keeps. My children would know the security of a loving home. Patricia trampled on my ideals. I despise the men who took advantage of her, as much as I despise her. People who have affairs are selfish go-getters. They don't care who gets hurt. They just want their way, with no ties, no responsibilities. In my book, they're the lowest of the low.'

His judging attitude horrified her. There wasn't the slightest hint of compassion or understanding in his words. The weaknesses of the human heart counted for nothing at all. How could she tell him about her affair with Richard, knowing that would define her as one of those he hardly counted among the human race?

To make matters worse, he was looking at her tenderly. 'It's hard for a girl like you to know what I mean. You're so honest, so direct. You couldn't comprehend the deceit some people build their lives on. Can you imagine what it must be like, sneaking, hiding, never being able to sit openly with the man you love, showing your true feelings?'

She was speechless. She knew only

too well how the constraints of an affair led to the kind of subterfuge he was describing. How often she'd made do with rushed visits, cancelled dates, rare outings where she'd had to hide her affection, not daring to hold Richard's hand in case they were seen. She knew about the loneliness and guilt. Will showed no understanding that affairs could happen between average people who did not anticipate any of the harm he seemed so sure about.

He mistook her silence. 'I can see you're shocked. Don't be. Nothing like that would ever come into your life. You're too clear-sighted.'

Caitlin was, now. She would never let such a situation occur again, after the pain she'd suffered over Richard. There was no use explaining that to Will. He had branded the people caught up in illicit passion and his fixed attitude gave no ground. She could never be honest with him. He would classify her as one of Patricia's kind, and she knew he would never run the risks of being hurt again. Her chest began to ache as though a tumor had lodged there. Love was supposed to overcome fear, yet she was too afraid to talk to Will about her past. And his own past hung between them like a dense, dusty curtain, dulling all the happiness they might have shared.

The drumming rain had eased. Slow, heavy drops gathered and dripped from the foliage.

'Ready to go?' He sprang up, offering his hand, and she followed obediently, the flattened grass soaking her shoes. Pausing at the gate, she cast one last look at the sweet little cottage where she'd let her wild imaginings link them, Will and herself, a couple risking a new start and building a retreat they could share. Her hopes dying, she walked slowly to the car.

The sky remained leaden, with little indication the day would clear.

Will was disappointed his plan to drive to some of the coastal beauty spots was spoiled, but Caitlin had lost interest in sightseeing.

'Let's look for somewhere to have lunch,' he suggested, apparently not noticing her despondency.

Being Sunday, many of the country restaurants were closed. Unconcerned, he drove on, eventually locating a place that catered for weekend custom and advertised antiques and curios along with its luncheon specialties.

'Would you like to have a look at their jewelry?' Will asked, while they waited to be served.

'I don't have much use for it.' It was a waste of time to go on with this relationship. It could only lead to heartbreak. She couldn't maintain a pretense of virtue. She didn't want him thinking of her as some kind of ideal woman, immunized against mistakes. His attitudes were harsh and unfeeling. What right had he, after all, to consider himself so much better than people who fell in love unwisely?

They were seated at a table near the window, which overlooked a peaceful rural scene. Horses grouped in pairs and trios moved aimlessly, cropping here and there. Following her gaze, Will suddenly reached over and covered her hand with his own.

'You're looking very lovely today,' he said with a smile. He was looking thoughtfully at her slender fingers as though taking their measurement.

It was tempting to respond, but she pulled her hand away. Didn't he realize that, holding himself aloof from commitment as he did, he could be as charming as he liked? To him, flirting might be a game, but girls like Angela mistook his attitude and took him seriously. Will hid behind his value judgments, using them just as he'd raised his shield with skill, blocking Tony's approach. It gave him an air of independence and power. Women would obviously be attracted to that, but nobody since Patricia had apparently touched his heart.

Startled by the air horn of a passing transport lorry, the horses broke into a gallop and surged forward as though overcome by the joy of living. Her heart warmed at the lovely rhythm of their stride as they stretched elegant necks and broke into some equine game. By the time the lunch was served — an assortment of fresh sandwiches, hot scones and pastries — her appetite had returned.

'Feeling better now?'

So he had noticed. 'I'm quite hungry. I didn't eat breakfast.'

'My lady should know better.' He looked approving as she helped herself to the appetizing food.

There was nothing she could do to heal the rift Will had unknowingly opened. She had to conceal her true self. That, or be honest, and he'd told her clearly how he would react to that. She might as well enjoy the remains of the day.

'I'm going to have a look at their display,' he said, as the waitress offered them hot towels and discreetly placed the bill facedown on the table. He walked over to cabinets where antique bracelets, pendants and rings were laid out on dark blue velvet. One glance at the price tags advised her they were items way out of her price range, but Will wasn't deterred.

'I have a young person with a birthday coming up. She's about your build. Mind trying a few pieces?'

She didn't believe his story for an instant. His intention to buy her a gift was touching, but she couldn't accept, under the circumstances. He asked to inspect a lovely silver bracelet and she offered her wrist unwillingly. Will did up the clasp. With the saleswoman standing right in front of them, she could hardly tell him why they had no future together. She made herself stare at the piece as though it held no appeal.

'It's rather heavy. I don't like bracelets, myself. They catch in everything and get in the way. But your young friend might like it.'

'I believe she would.' He was quite at ease, maintaining the subterfuge. 'Anyone would appreciate the quality of this, and there's room to have it engraved.' He pointed at the display case. 'What about those? Do they please my lady?'

Sensing a sale, the woman quickly drew out a stand of magnificently-set rings. Judging Caitlin's fit, she thrust a ruby and diamond circle onto her ring finger, exclaiming that it looked perfect on her slim hand. So it did. Caitlin dragged it off.

'I'm not looking to buy jewelry today,' she informed the woman firmly, and walked away from the counter. She found a showing of local paintings in a side alcove, and went to inspect them, leaving Will to make whatever explanation he liked.

One picture, of a run-down miner's cottage in a paddock of dry-looking grass, appealed. Impulsively she decided to buy the little memento of a day she knew she would never forget. Back home, at least she'd have this image of a country cottage half-buried in summer growth, to remind her of a love that never had a chance to flower.

5

In the car, Will watched as she unwrapped the canvas.

'Quaint.'

He sounded polite. She knew it was an amateur work but its artistic merit was secondary to the memories it would hold.

'I like it.'

He didn't offer to show her his own purchase. Well, if he'd refused to take her hint and had bought the bracelet anyway, he would have to think of someone else to give it to.

'Do you want to go home?'

'I think so.' Storm clouds warned the downpour was about to start again. It was no weather for sightseeing. Already the humid air misted the windows, enclosing them in a steamy cocoon of privacy. It would be so easy to snuggle close to him and raise her face to his kisses. In many ways, Will was any woman's fantasy — handsome, rich, intelligent, caring. But today she'd seen he was also hurt and unforgiving. If she told him the truth about her past, his anger would be frightening. She dared not risk it. The longer she spent with him, the harder it would be to say goodbye.

He pulled smoothly onto the freeway, heading back to Sydney.

'My place or yours?'

His light tone always left him a loophole to pretend their relationship was strictly casual. She knew he desired her. She only had to give him the signal. But remembering his massage, and the way his skilled hands had sent erotic shivers through her body, she knew she would be unable to resist him. She had to be strong.

'I have a headache. I should go back to Heather's.'

It was the weakest excuse and he raised his eyebrows but said nothing. In fact she did feel drained. She needed to be alone, to sort out the painful conflict troubling her. Perhaps Heather would have words of wise counsel. Closing her eyes, she rested her head back on the luxurious leather. She could block out his image that way, but the psychic link between them remained strong. She was sure he was dwelling on memories of Patricia. If only he would talk about her openly, instead of brooding! But it was not for her to keep raising that topic. He had a right to privacy, after all.

Drivers were starting to use their headlights as the rain began again in earnest. Soon the rhythm of the windscreen wipers joined Will's selection of CDs, filling the silence between them as they drove south.

When he arrived back at her sister's, he made no move to come inside.

'Thank you for the day.'

'My pleasure. No doubt I'll see you soon.'

Caitlin ran through the drizzle to the porch and watched him drive away. Her tight throat swallowed the warning that she'd thrown away an opportunity, though for what, she wasn't sure.

Heather was surprised to see her home so early.

'I expected you to make the most of your chances!'

She intended her remark as a joke but Caitlin snapped, 'I'm not Will's type.'

'What do you mean? He's smitten with you!'

'He told me what he thinks of people who have affairs.'

'And you had to explain about Richard?'

'How could I? He's put me on a pedestal. As long as I have to stay there, we're not going anywhere.'

Tears of frustration overflowed and Heather spoke gently. 'Then step off the pedestal. Tell him what happened.'

'I can't!' It was no use. Heather hadn't heard his bitter tone or seen the angry judgment in his expression. 'You're right about one thing, Heather.

He's still involved with his ex. It's hate, not love. Still . . . '

'Opposite sides of the coin, you mean?'

'Exactly. I don't know how he can deal with it. I just know he'll never risk falling in love again, until he's free.'

'I thought he was on the verge of just that, with you.'

'On the verge, perhaps. But that's not enough, is it?' Her sister's arms were comforting, and she began to cry in earnest.

'Wait and see. That's all I can advise. Now let's have a cup of tea. We've had a ghastly morning here, with the neighbors.'

Caitlin was relieved to change the subject, and Heather wanted to defuse the unpleasant scene next door. 'I'll be so pleased when they move.' She was slapping mugs and banging biscuit tins as though they were the offending neighbors. 'Their dog ran away again. Then the girls found it in our yard and hid it. Tony took it home. Of course it copped another hiding and the girls heard all the shouting and yelping. They were dreadfully upset.'

'It's not right. Why don't you report them?'

'I rang the council months ago. They said as long as the animal has food and water, they can't intervene.'

'When are they moving?'

'Next weekend, I believe. Good riddance.'

'Yes. Out of sight, out of mind.' Caitlin hated animal abuse.

Heather gave her sister a sharp look. 'We can't mend all the problems in the world,' she pointed out.

Caitlin drank her tea in silence. Heather was right, of course. Only Will could solve the problem of his memories.

Heather guessed the trend of her sister's one-track mind. 'There isn't a perfect man walking the earth, you know. It's so easy to dwell on the faults.'

'But what can I do?'

'Love helps you see the best in people.'

'I can see the best in Will.' But her sister did not understand. To ignore what she'd learned about him today could only make the eventual parting more painful. She stood up and placed her half-empty mug in the sink. 'I'm going to lie down for a while.'

She left Heather gazing after her, looking concerned.

* * *

During the next few days, Caitlin was grateful for the busy family atmosphere, where there was little time to sit and brood. In Heather and Tony's household there was always something going on. Visitors, phone calls, impromptu outings and the demands of two children kept her anchored in the everyday world. Each time the phone rang, her heart started to pound and a mixture of anticipation and dread made her feel almost ill. But Will did not attempt to get in touch with her. She reasoned it was better that way. He'd only been in her life a short time, and she'd managed perfectly well without him until now. She tried to cast him as unavailable, another Richard, in effect still bound to another woman.

Heather noticed her sister's brittle light-heartedness. She said nothing. Caitlin took Jackie and Katy walking around the suburb, and helped with housework and meals. At night she sat staring at television shows, her glazed expression suggesting her mind was far away, until an unexpected event turned the whole household upside down.

She woke after another hot, restless night, and lay trying to ignore the familiar strains of an argument next door, when the ringing of the phone set off her usual discomfort. If that was Will, suggesting they should meet . . . but hope trailed away when, as usual, the call was not for her.

She heard a muffled conversation, followed by an uncharacteristic whoop. Heather burst into the room.

'You won't believe this!'

'What's happened?'

'We've won a holiday! Tony and I have won a trip north!'

Heather had taken part in a promotion at the local mall, where buyers deposited their purchase dockets in a barrel and were entered in a draw. It was a popular form of advertising in Australia, with everything from cornflakes to cars being promoted with these lucky prize schemes. Heather apparently entered every competition that came her way. Her docket had been drawn and the prize was a ten-day tropical island holiday for two, with all expenses paid. Heather was so excited she'd flushed bright red, until, remembering the children, she sighed.

'Of course, we won't be able to go. Can you imagine Jackie and Katy in an exclusive tourist hotel, spilling orange juice on the tablecloth and tumbling into the pool?'

Caitlin had made up her mind as soon as she'd heard the news. 'You're going and that's that.' No one deserved such a piece of luck more than Heather and Tony. They were far from wealthy, yet their own generous offer had given Caitlin this holiday. Now fortune had brought them a similar reward, and Caitlin's presence was the very factor that would make their trip possible.

'I'm going to mind the girls while you and Tony take your prize.' Caitlin's tone was determined and Heather's face lit up with hope.

'How can we just go off and leave you alone? It wouldn't be fair.'

'I wouldn't be alone. The girls would keep me occupied. Don't you see, I miss them both. This will be the perfect chance for us to get to know one another properly. I was a stranger to them when I arrived and they're the only family I have, apart from you. Let me mind them? I'd love to. You'd be crazy to pass up an opportunity like this.'

'I know. We'd never afford a holiday like this on Tony's wages.' Tony drove for a firm of couriers and his single income was soon eroded by daily living expenses.

'And you'll have another member of the family before long.' Caitlin sensed she was close to persuading her sister.

'True. Once the baby's born we can forget holidays for a good while.'

'Then it's settled. I'll look after Jackie and Katy.'

Seeing Caitlin's determined expression, Heather capitulated.

'I'm going to wake Tony and tell him the good news. And I'll have to go through my clothes. What does one pack for a tropical paradise?'

The next few days were pleasantly chaotic. Tony and Heather realized Caitlin was not putting on an act when she insisted spending time with the girls would deepen their bond. Jackie and Katy were equally keen. Their young aunt often took them to their favorite places — the playground, the toyshop and the store where they could buy little bags of sweets.

The trip would have to be taken

immediately, while Caitlin was available and Tony still on his Christmas break. Remembering her excitement when she'd been plunged into the whirl of preparations for her own impromptu trip, Caitlin helped her sister as she dusted off suitcases, moaned at the shabby state of her clothes and rushed off to the post-Christmas sales to try on a few new summer outfits. Heather made endless lists, ranging from doctors' and hospital addresses to emergency treatments for snake or spider bites and bee stings.

'I'll leave this list on the fridge. But if you're worried, promise you'll ring me straight away and I'll come home.'

'Of course.' But Caitlin smiled to herself. As an experienced nurse, she thought she could cope adequately with anything that could happen to a couple of healthy children, but she admired Heather's devotion. Her sister had never had a break in the eight years since Jackie was born. The holiday would be just what she needed to remember the lost romance of her courtship days.

Visualizing beach and forest walks, romantic sunset dinners, nightclubs, shows and the complete relief from everyday duties, Caitlin occasionally drifted into daydreams where she and Will were in a similar setting. She pulled herself up whenever this happened. Dwelling on memories set off that bruised ache in her heart, reminding her just how deeply he affected her emotions.

To add to the disruption, Tony remembered he'd asked a group of friends to the house, partly for a planning session to do with the annual Saint Valentine's masked ball, held in early February. This year, Tony was to act as coordinator. He'd casually invited everyone to stay afterwards for a barbecue, which he only thought to mention the day beforehand. Heather flew into a panic while Tony seemed to think people would be satisfied with a sausage on a piece of bread. At the last minute, he was sent to the supermarket to buy enough steak and sausages to feed a small army. Caitlin and Heather opened tins and made salads, and several people phoned with offers to bring cakes or desserts. By the time their friends were due to arrive, the barbecue and outdoor furniture were set up and bottles of drink were standing neck-deep in crushed ice.

Caitlin went to change her shorts and T-shirt for something more in keeping with a party. She'd spent the afternoon in the kitchen, helping prepare pizzas, sandwiches and snacks. It was a relief to wash away the sticky grime of her culinary efforts under a cool shower. She was starting to adjust to the heat. Apart from the annoying mosquitoes and flies, summer living in Australia was a delightfully relaxed mood. She'd soon learned to smear her arms and legs with the insect repellent that, to begin with, gave everyone their odd chemical aroma. She hardly noticed that now. The long evenings, extended by daylight saving, remained light until after eight o'clock, and by then a cool breeze had often begun to dissipate the day's heat.

She chose one of her favorite dresses, of freshly-ironed yellow cotton, and applied makeup with care. A necklace and earrings added the finishing touch. Jackie and Katy watched the preparations with approval, begging to try Caitlin's nail polish and lipstick. Seeing the serious way Jackie instructed Katy to hold out her grubby paws with their minute nails, Caitlin looked forward to the coming time with her nieces. They would forge a lasting bond and the busy routine would save her from thinking about Will and wondering whether she should have settled for a few white lies about her past. What had it to do with him?

But she couldn't ignore the need to be honest. For the past few days she hadn't mentioned him and she was glad Heather did not probe. Talking about him stirred up memories that made her long to re-establish contact.

* * *

Tony was in his element — hospitable and noisy as the guests began to arrive, carrying small children, plates of food or cartons of beer. The kitchen soon overflowed with food and drink, and chip packets and empty cans began to litter the rooms Heather had tidied. The backyard changed to a playing field where kids of assorted ages and sizes raced about.

With every new knock at the door, Caitlin's heart gave a jolt. Will's presence at the party had not been discussed and she'd been too proud to enquire whether he'd be coming. She had no idea whether he was even in Sydney. Perhaps his business had taken him off somewhere. The thought that he was out of reach made her feel bereft. What if he'd really interpreted her withdrawn moods as a clear signal that she didn't want to see him again? He would be used to girls who liked his playful flattery and responded to his charm. He'd probably decided Caitlin was a bore or, worse, a tease. She should have risked confronting him with her past affair. He might have a set of standards in theory but perhaps in reality he'd be less harsh. Now she would never have the chance to find out.

Tony was not the type of chairman to allow interminable meetings, and gathered his impromptu committee in one room to allocate tasks for the ball and plan the theme of the evening. Business dealt with, he ordered everyone to enjoy themselves as much as he and Heather intended to do in their tropical hideaway; for good measure, throwing in the announcement that their third child was on the way. With so much to celebrate, the gathering took on renewed enthusiasm.

Caitlin found herself chatting to one of the younger members, Martin, who sidled to stand beside her. He was good-looking, perhaps nineteen or twenty, with a shy manner. He seemed at a loss in the noisy crowd and her maternal instinct surfaced.

'Who are you here with tonight?'

'Just myself.' He sounded lonely. 'I was hoping to see someone but she's not here.'

He went on to explain one of the girls in the group had raised his hopes that she would go out with him. He seemed to have fallen in love, adding in a dismal way, 'I think she prefers someone else.'

His rather hapless acceptance made Caitlin ask, 'But have you really checked that out with her?'

'I can't ask her outright. She might laugh.'

'Faint heart never won fair lady.' She realized she'd taken a similarly apathetic stand with Will. Opening your heart and risking rejection was never easy to do.

However, Martin was only too ready to describe the charms of the particular lady he fancied. He was a born romantic, ready to shower his lady love with red roses and verses. Caitlin hoped the girl would be the type to respond. She sounded self-centered, as though liking the idea of several suitors she could keep on a string.

'She was chosen as the princess in our recent coronation. But she wasn't available on the night.'

'Would her name be Angela?' Caitlin had made the connection and Martin beamed.

'Isn't it a beautiful name?'

He looked so hopeful. Caitlin did not mention the unfortunate phone call that had almost wrecked her trust in Will.

'Yes, a lovely name,' she agreed as a hand fell on her shoulder. She turned and saw Will, his expression masked.

Overwhelming relief flooded her. Without admitting it, she'd made all her careful preparations with the hope that he would attend. The same advice she'd been about to offer Martin was now squarely back on her shoulders. He wasn't a mind-reader. She had to be honest and tell him why she was afraid. She had to give him the chance to accept her, and that included her life before they'd met. She did not blame Will for his past mistakes. Why assume he would judge her? They deserved the chance to start afresh.

She made no attempt to hide her pleasure at seeing him.

'I didn't know you were coming tonight.'

Will nodded to Martin, whom he evidently knew. 'The last few days have been chaos. Some of the house piers are in such bad condition I have a major structural crisis on my hands. I've been grubbing under the veranda, hoping the whole thing wouldn't collapse on top of me.'

He did look disheveled, as though he'd barely taken time to change his shirt and run a comb through his hair.

'I can't stay long. An engineer mate's coming round to discuss salvage operations.'

'It's still good to see you.' Caitlin was

so elated he'd made the effort to come that she felt like kissing him in front of the whole gathering. He smiled down at her, the attractive lines around his eyes deepening.

'Likewise, my lady.' He did not conceal how desirable he found her in her summery yellow dress. He paused, glancing at Martin who was looking on, a wistful expression etched on his youthful features.

'Am I interrupting anything?' There was an abrupt note to Will's query and Caitlin almost broke into laughter. Surely he couldn't think she was interested in the lovesick young man?

'Martin,' she said, determined there would be no misunderstandings, 'I know you'll excuse me now. Will and I have a few things to discuss.'

'I'm sorry. Don't mean to be in the way.' He wandered away.

'Poor boy! He's having romantic troubles.' She spoke lightly, but Will wasn't amused.

'I hear you are going to be mother

while Tony and Heather are away?'

No doubt her sister had told him when she issued the invitation to the gathering.

'Yes. They deserve a break. I'm very pleased. I'll get to know my nieces better.'

'Then everyone will benefit. Caitlin, the only reason I'm here is to talk to you. Can we find somewhere private?' The noise in the room was making it hard to be heard. Together they wove their way through the groups, instinctively seeking a quiet corner.

'What did you want to talk about?' As if she needed to ask! Now the moment was here, her body was sending uncomfortable messages; fear in the pit of her stomach, desire when she stood close to him and breathed in his scent, relief that the truth would soon be out in the open, for better or for worse. Could he hear her heart thumping? Her pulse was racing as he looked deep into her eyes. He must feel very much as she did — finding his orderly plans upended by a stranger. He must wonder about the lure of retaining an independent life.

'To tell you the truth, you confuse me.'

It seemed Will was ready to pry open her most vulnerable memories. His expression was veiled in the fading light. Was there something cautious in his eyes, as though even one offhand remark would make him walk away? She remembered his cutting phrases. *Selfish go-getters, the lowest of the low.* What if he turned in disgust, and left her standing there in front of all the guests? Suddenly she had a wild impulse to run away.

'Will, I do want to talk to you.' She laid her small hand on his arm appealingly. 'But not here. Not tonight. It's not the place.'

As if confirming her words, children raced past them, shrill voices drowning out his reply.

He waited until they had moved on. 'Phone me then,' was all he said. Caitlin watched him make his excuses and leave.

For the rest of the evening, as she talked to strangers and helped serve supper, she felt she was on the edge of some big change in her life. She knew it was connected with the man who had appeared in her life on New Year's Eve. He'd swept away every orderly pattern she thought she needed. The uncertainty and fluctuating emotions that had made her so unlike her normal self could only mean one thing. For better or for worse, she was in love with Will. She could only follow wherever that was leading her, toward an upheaval she could never have imagined even two weeks ago. He had a power over her and there was nothing she could do about it.

Sensing the truth of her thoughts, she shivered. The story she had to tell him could bring out a side of Will she never wanted to face. She dreaded having to tell him she was no different from his ex-wife, or from the men who had casual affairs with a married woman — people he despised and disowned. His face might set in cold rejection. He might turn and walk away from her forever. But to live a lie was not her nature. Will would have to accept her past or let her go.

She was relieved when people began to leave. The party had lost all appeal for her since Will had left. He was part of her now, entangled in her thoughts and emotions. Forgetting him, if that had to happen, would be impossible.

6

Once Heather and Tony left on their holiday, the household quickly formed a new routine. Jackie and Katy saw their parents' absence as an opportunity too good to overlook, and demanded stories, games and special treats that Heather would have dealt with sternly. However, Caitlin felt she could indulge her nieces; after all, they'd never been separated from their mother or father. A favorite aunt wasn't quite the same. She allowed them their demands, which lasted well after bedtime. Katy gave in first. She fell asleep on the carpet, thumb in mouth. By the time Jackie had assisted with the tucking-up process and agreed to go to bed herself, Caitlin had realized how demanding it must be to attend to the needs of small children every day of one's life. No wonder Heather was sometimes short-tempered, and entertained dreams of freedom once the children were at school.

Everything had its price. Domestic security and companionship were balanced by duty. Curled up on the sofa, Caitlin came to the conclusion that it would depend entirely on who shared that scenario with you. She could imagine Will, lying back there, his long legs slung over the armrest, his expression inviting her to join him for a quiet evening alone with him.

He'd asked her to phone him. She rehearsed various ways to tell him the facts of her past, always stopping when her apprehension was too much to deal with. Several times she'd tried to face her fears and ring him. She'd pressed in his number, panicked and cut the connection. With dread she visualized his look of disgust as he stood up and walked away from her. She knew quite well that, if he did do that, he was certainly the wrong man for her, but that did nothing at all to settle her nerves.

It was nearly midnight. Silence issued from the girls' room. Far too late to disturb Will. Or was it? She couldn't stand the waiting any longer and punched in his number. His voice came through as clearly as if he was sitting right there beside her. Had he been waiting for her call?

'Caitlin? I hoped it would be you.' There was no mistaking his pleasure.

'I know it's late. It took me ages to persuade the girls to go to bed.'

He chuckled. 'Working the scene, eh? Smart kids. Don't worry, I'm not busy.'

His voice, warm and masculine, seemed to wrap itself around her, encouraging her to be open with him. She thought she'd only have to say the word and he'd be in his car and on his way to see her at once. But that wasn't what she had in mind — not when the house was a mess, her appearance was decidedly casual, and she was worn out after her first day alone with her nieces. No, she had a better plan in mind.

'I'd like to invite you to dinner.'

'Tomorrow?' He sounded eager.

'Say the day after? The girls have already extracted a promise from me to take them to the pool in the morning. They have a bus trip lined up too. I'd never manage to cook for you, after all that.'

'So you're going to make me wait again?' He tried a light tone but she sensed he must be missing her.

'Will, I'm really not playing games. I promised the girls, that's all. We'll be able to talk soon.'

'Then I'll just have to await my lady's pleasure.'

She appreciated that he was willing to let her make the rules for their next meeting. They both knew it would be a turning point. Perhaps that was why she wanted to have time to prepare, with candlelight, a romantic table setting, and a good wine. Not to mention herself, dressed to please, her hair and makeup impeccable.

'I promise you I'll make the evening

special. Tell me, did you solve your problem with the piers?'

Will outlined his plan and she asked several questions, wanting to keep their contact going. He had a subtle way of turning the conversation back to her own interests. By the time they ended the call, she realized they'd been talking for nearly an hour. How quickly time passed when you were with the man you desired!

She must have fallen asleep as soon as her head touched the pillow. She'd faced her reluctance to be honest with Will. Very soon, with luck, their conflict would fade away and they would be free to explore their relationship and discover its deeper meaning.

* * *

The early-morning racket pulled her from deep sleep. A large furniture removal truck was backing in to the next-door drive. So this must be moving day. Heather had told her the neighbors were leaving soon. Good riddance!

Breakfast and a perfunctory brush with dishes and laundry occupied the next couple of hours. The girls were nagging her to get ready for the pool, when Martin's hopeful voice sounded through the open door.

'Anybody home?'

Of course they were home. Martin wasn't the intrusive type, to just march inside without an invitation. Surely he knew Heather and Tony were away? Why had he decided to visit now?

'I'm just returning the fighter's equipment.' He dropped a heavy shield and sword on the floor.

'We're about to go out, Martin.' She was ready to hustle him out the door, but Jackie ran out, demanding a game, and Katy imitated her sister. They soon had Martin clambering round the house on all fours, bellowing and making ferocious attacks from behind doors and under tables, while the children raced about, screaming and thoroughly enjoying themselves. It was good of Martin to bother. He diverted their chatter so she could get on with packing the picnic lunch, but she was already running late.

'I think you should go and put on your swimmers now,' she said firmly. 'If we miss the bus, we'll have to wait another hour.'

'I can give you all a lift to the pool.'

'Are you sure?' She was grateful. He'd saved her from lugging a heavy bag plus two live wires to the bus stop, and he seemed pleased he could help. Perhaps he was at a loose end while friends were on holiday. In any case, he wasn't a man to distract her for long. She soon forgot him once they arrived at the swimming baths and she found supervising the girls was a full-time occupation. She had no chance to swim even one length of the pool herself.

Getting them out of the water was a protracted battle as they kept pleading for just one more dip. Even getting dressed was fraught with unexpected delays. Jackie had lost her favorite headband and complained loudly until Caitlin promised they would go to the chemist shop and buy her another one. Katy put her pants on upside down and waddled up and down the changing shed, both legs stuck in the one hole and a puzzled look on her face. As Caitlin laughed and helped dislodge her from her strait-jacket, she was beginning to understand why it took Heather so long to get small jobs done.

They had their picnic under shady trees near the pool enclosure. The girls were flushed and she hoped she'd been generous enough with the sunscreen. Her sister's trust had pleased her, but knowing she was suddenly responsible for two ready-made nieces was a worrying thought. It might be different, growing with one's children on a leisurely day-by-day basis. But how did mothers ever develop the confidence to let children out of sight? There were so many hazards! Traffic, deep water, snakes and spiders, falls, cuts, uncontrolled dogs, rusty nails — who knew what potential dangers could create havoc in an instant? While Heather and Tony luxuriated in a spa or sipped cocktails in some elegant bar, she had to learn the role of mother with no gentle introductory period.

'Let's go home now and all have an afternoon rest,' she suggested, without success, as the girls raised cries of protest and reminded her she'd promised them a bus ride in to the city. At such a young age, they were shrewd enough to know their aunt would not deliver the firm veto or exasperated smack they could expect if their mother was in charge.

Caitlin gathered the damp towels and bathers, packed the picnic hamper and they trudged to the bus stop. Jackie complained she had a prickle in her toe. Katy wanted to be carried over the hot tarmac, complaining her sandals stuck to the melting bitumen. The wait for a city bus seemed to go on forever. She bundled the grizzling pair aboard, where they both demanded to sit beside her. The three squeezed in to a double seat, the girls wriggling and jostling as first they wanted to sit on Caitlin's knee, then argued over who could have the window seat.

The bus wound its way interminably. Caitlin had no idea where they were, as nondescript suburbs drifted past. In her haste to board, she hadn't even taken notice of where the bus was headed. All they could do was to wait until they reached the terminus and then come back on the return trip. That might take hours. Already Katy wanted to go to the toilet and Jackie said she felt sick. Hot and squashed between the irritable pair, Caitlin began to count the days until Heather was due to return home.

Eventually the bus reached its destination. The driver directed her to public toilets and told her she had fifteen minutes before the return journey. They were at the beach front. A cool sea breeze blew and the expanse of restless ocean soothed her. Somewhere in the invisible distance lay New Zealand. In only a few more weeks, she would be airborne, gazing down on that shimmering water separating her from her only family. This time was precious, however trying the girls might be. Her mood changed to mellow enjoyment of the present.

'Come on. We'll use the toilets, then buy an ice cream over there at the kiosk.'

She did not bother to deliver a lecture as the girls' clothing and hands were soon covered in vanilla-scented stickiness. On the ride home, Jackie peacefully gazed out the window while Katy collapsed in sleepy surrender against Caitlin. Her niece's flushed face and chubby arms rested so trustingly against her body. Love filled her. She could understand how mothers could accommodate the unrelenting needs of their offspring. Katy's silky tangles of hair and rounded cheeks retained traces of babyhood, but already Jackie's limbs had the thinner lines of a girl.

Before Caitlin could add up the passing of the years, her nieces would be young women, ready to go out on dates, get married and start families of their own. She was twenty-four now. What would it be like to be a wife, running her home, sharing life with her man, raising a family? For the rest of the trip, she fell into a daydream, inhabited by Will.

As the trio wearily made their way home, a removal van passed them. So the neighbors had finally gone. That was a cause for celebration. The rest of the day passed quickly. She had a meal to plan, two grubby girls to bathe, and stories to read. Heather phoned long distance, to make sure all was well at home. Reassured, she described the resort in glowing words.

'They gave us the red-carpet treatment as soon as we stepped off the plane. A limo took us to the resort and we had champagne and chocolates waiting for us in the suite.'

Caitlin allowed herself a smile as she privately compared her day with Heather's.

'Everything went smoothly here,' she reported. Her sister deserved this holiday. 'What's the resort like?'

'Fantastic! The water's so clear you can see the sandy bottom, and the gardens are like paradise. We're going dancing tonight, there's a great band and guest entertainment.' As an afterthought, she added, 'What are your plans?'

'I'm afraid they don't include champagne! The girls have worn me out.'

She described the outing, making it sound as amusing as she could. No way would she admit how tired she was, nor that she wished her sister would hurry home and take up the reins of her smoothly-run household. Heather was clearly on a high.

'Tomorrow Tony's going scuba diving and we'll view the reef through a glass-bottomed boat.'

'Sounds amazing!'

By now the girls had realized who was on the phone and were clamoring to speak to their mother. After they'd chatted both were restless, reminded that Heather was far away. Caitlin had to re-read the stories she'd already read once, and eventually she resorted to a sharp tone of voice, at which they climbed obediently into bed like dutiful angels. Even their favorite aunt had her limits, it seemed, and they accepted her firm goodnight cuddle with no more protests.

Silence descended. Caitlin lay back on the old sofa with a sigh of relief. For her first try at being a mother, she'd done pretty well, she thought. But if this had been a typical day, she hadn't had a single minute to herself. Tomorrow was the special dinner with Will. It might be wise to make sure her dress was pressed, and she wanted to condition her hair and do her nails. Forcing herself out of her brief relaxation, she set up the ironing board and iron. While it was heating, she applied the conditioning treatment she'd been saving for a special occasion, winding a plastic bag around her head like a scarf as the instructions advised. Just as she picked up the iron, there was a knock at the door. For a moment she had a horrified impression that Will was paying a surprise visit. She was inclined to look about for someplace to hide, until the foolishness of that thought struck home and she went reluctantly to answer the door.

But it was only Martin who stood on the porch, not seeming at all surprised by her appearance. She was asking herself why he'd called in for the second time that day, when he thrust out Jackie's headband.

'I found this in my car.'

It was a feeble excuse, she thought. 'I won't invite you in,' she said firmly. 'I'm dead tired and just heading off to bed.'

Whatever he wanted — coffee, a heart-to-heart about Angela, merely the company of another single person to while away a lonely evening — she did not intend to encourage him. Perhaps he was used to dropping in unannounced, for Tony was popular with all the young men in the society. She was about to say goodnight when she saw beside him the black dog from next door. His brown eyes fixed on her and his tail gave a hopeful wag.

'He was sitting at your gate.' Martin had noticed the direction of her gaze. 'Are you minding him?'

'Certainly not! He belongs to the neighbors but they moved today.'

'Then why's he still here?'

The dog, aware he was under discussion, watched silently, his body language suggesting he would run like lightning if anyone made a threatening gesture.

'Perhaps they couldn't fit him in and they're coming back for him,' Martin said.

'Or they've abandoned him.' She felt a sinking feeling in the pit of her stomach. *They wouldn't . . . surely . . .* There were shelters to leave an animal while it was rehoused. But this poor thin creature looked homeless as it stared from one human to the other, as though trying to interpret their strange language.

'Surely not!' Instinctively Martin patted the docile animal. 'He does seem hungry.'

'I shouldn't feed him. You know what they say about strays. They'll keep coming if you give them food.'

If only Martin would spirit the poor creature away! But he looked as worried as she felt.

'I live in a flat and we're not allowed pets.'

Helpless, they stood staring down at the animal.

'I wonder what breed he is,' said Caitlin.

'Part Border Collie, maybe a bit of Labrador. Who knows what else?'

The dog, sensing he was under discussion, sat up very straight as though claiming impeccable lineage.

'Let's leave it till the morning,

Martin. I'm sure the people will be back for him by then.' She remembered her sister's allergy and added, 'But if the girls see him, they'll beg to keep him. We'll have to keep it secret while we work out what to do.'

'Sure. Our secret! I'll stop by tomorrow and see whether the owners did come back. Quite frankly, I'll be surprised if they do.'

'I'm sure he'll be quite all right for tonight.'

'Bye, fella.' Martin gave the dog a pat. Caitlin waved him off and closed the door, but the image of the animal's hopeful eyes was too hard to forget. After ten minutes, she couldn't help herself; she found a can of tuna in the cupboard and took it outside, where the dog lay patiently on the path.

'Here, take this and go away!'

Tipping the mess of fish on a patch of grass, she refused to allow herself the pleasure of watching the dog demolish his impromptu supper. She was far too soft to get involved here. Heather would be furious if she came back to find the neighbors' dog in residence. However unpleasant and belligerent the people had been, surely they weren't so cruel as to simply drive away, leaving the animal to whatever fate befell it?

Feeling guilty that she'd virtually given the dog an invitation to stay, she finished ironing her low-cut red dress, then washed the treatment cream out of her hair. She still needed to think of every detail that would add up to a perfect dinner for two. She could not find any candles or a candle-holder, and added the items to her shopping list. In the back of the linen cupboard she unearthed one of Heather's trousseau tablecloths, obviously hidden from the rigors of family meals. There were matching serviettes, and a couple of long-stemmed crystal glasses survived in a high cupboard. Heather wouldn't mind this invasion of her personal belongings, for such a good cause.

The meal still had to be planned. There were plenty of recipes in the women's magazines lying around. For half an hour, Caitlin browsed through photographs of banquets of style and elegance, flavored with Moroccan spices and Asian sauces that Heather was unlikely to have in her pantry. Her marketing veered more toward ice cream cones, children's breakfast cereals and barbecue condiments. The shopping list was growing. Caitlin was planning to spend as much on this single dinner as her sister probably spent in an entire week. The wine alone was bound to cost plenty. Will wouldn't complain if she provided a bargain-bin special, but she was determined to give him nothing but the best. Their future together might depend on the outcome of this evening. If he saw her looking her best, and realized what a good hostess and excellent cook she could be, his mood would be mellow. He would listen amiably and decide it was the future that mattered, not her past, nor his own.

Caitlin gave her nails a manicure. Yawning widely, she still had to settle on a choice for background music. Tony and Heather's music was dated and the CDs looked the worse for wear. After a fruitless search through groups that had probably accompanied them through their courting days, she added music to her list. She would try to buy that CD Will kept in his car. Surely he would understand her message then?

* * *

Gray skies and a weather forecast of afternoon thunderstorms did nothing to dull her anticipation the next morning. To her relief, the dog was gone. Most likely the owners had come and collected him first thing. Glad she'd organized herself, she hurried the girls through breakfast, planning to set out to the shops early. The housework could be done later. If they walked far enough on their outing, perhaps her two little charges would agree to have a rest while she vacuumed and tidied. They were excited by the idea of a special dinner, though Caitlin made sure they understood she and Will would not be sharing their meal with anyone else.

'It's special,' she explained, and when Katy asked, 'What's special?' Jackie said smugly, 'Silly, it's when people are going to get engaged.'

'What's engaged?'

Caitlin hastily said it was nothing of the sort — just the kind of food children didn't like to eat.

'But you can have your favorite meal early,' she promised. 'Now hurry up and get ready.'

The shopping excursion seemed to take twice as long as she'd expected. Even a simple trip to the shops involved searching for lost sandals, settling of disputes, attending to minor accidents and turning back at the gate for yet another toilet stop. The day had that sultry feel they all found tiring. Soon their faces were beaded in perspiration.

The girls' pace seemed interminably slow. They had to stop to watch a train, then a bee caught in a spider's web. Katy stubbed her toe. Jackie, not to be outdone, insisted there was a stone in her sandal. She refused to budge, hopping about complaining of the hot pavement while Caitlin carried out a fruitless search, pointing out a small bump in the liner that might have been uncomfortable.

For the rest of the walk, Jackie hobbled pointedly, going even slower than before. Caitlin decided they would go home by taxi, regardless of expense. She had no desire to serve a half-raw dinner. At this rate, it would be afternoon by the time all the shopping was completed.

She hadn't reckoned on taking two children through a packed supermarket where the lower-level shelves were loaded with toys, sweets and nursery-tale DVDs. Nor had she expected that a request for candles would produce large, church-like objects useful in a blackout, but hardly the type to decorate a dinner table with. She had to trudge from shop to shop, before eventually finding an expensive candelabrum with complementary twisted candles at a jeweler's. Nobody had heard of the CD she'd hoped to buy. She searched the bargain bins in vain, until Katy finally picked a disc because she liked the cover picture.

Worn out by the frustrations of shopping and the grizzles of the weary children, she took them to a coffee shop, where Katy dropped her iced cake on the floor, bent to pick it up and knocked over her juice. When Caitlin wouldn't let her eat the cake she broke into loud sobs while sedate people at other tables stared as though suspecting child abuse.

A sudden shattering roll of thunder distracted the children, but made a lot of shoppers decide to go home by taxi, rather than risk a soaking. The queue was already halfway round the corner by the time Caitlin found the rank and lugged all the parcels, plus her charges, into the line. Her mind was racing with revised plans. She wouldn't have time now to make the mousse. It might not set. And that thyme roast chicken with cranberry stuffing took a lot of preparation. She wished she hadn't left the housework. How would she ever have time to supervise the girls, clean up, prepare a three-course dinner and attend to her own appearance before Will arrived? No wonder Heather became grumpy at times. At the moment, a civilized holiday resort sounded like heaven.

As the taxi arrived home, she heard a joyful barking. The dog bounded down the neighboring path toward the car. With a feeling of dread in her chest, she shooed it away, but it had already taken her measure and merely backed off several feet, sat down and twitched its ears alertly.

'Go home!' she shouted, hoping the girls did not realize the poor creature no longer had a home. Fortunately, the storm broke just then and the dog ran back to hide under the abandoned house. Stumbling inside with her bags, she now had the prospect of two damp and hungry children to amuse until the downpour eased. It was impossible to do any cleaning, and the cooking preparations were constantly interrupted. The menu went through more than one revision as time ticked by at an alarming rate. Canned soup would have to do instead of homemade. The elaborate dessert she'd planned to serve with fresh fruit salad had to be forgotten. At least she had the prawn cocktails chilling, along with Will's favorite wine. She wasn't a wine buff and was still doubting the price of the ordinary-looking bottle the salesman had brought out from some special room, handling it respectfully. As far as she cared, cask wine was as good as vintage; but as long as Will was pleased, she would be.

She was determined to have a bath, even if it meant locking the girls in the bathroom with her. She rushed from room to room, picking up obvious mess and hoping Will wouldn't notice all the chores she'd had to leave undone. She still had to prepare a separate dinner for the children, though that would just be sausages and chips. She would leave her makeup and dress until the girls were both fed and bathed, ready for an early night. They seemed to understand her wish to spend the evening alone with Will and promised they'd go to bed without a fuss as soon as they were told.

* * *

She'd clearly said that dinner would not be until seven o'clock. When there was a firm knock, just as she was draining the chips, she guessed Martin was trying one of his impromptu visits again. She went to send him on his way, her expression the one she used for salesmen and religious visitors.

Will stood smiling on the porch, a

magnificent sheaf of red roses in his arms.

Caitlin stared at him, her hair bedraggled, her shirt stained with grease splashes. Will did not seem at all put out by her appearance. He held out the bouquet and she accepted the flowers, wishing she could bury her face in the fragrant blooms and hide.

'You're early!'

'I couldn't wait any longer to see you.'

She should have been pleased, except that nothing had happened as she'd planned. Her vision of an immaculate house, sweet sleepy children tucked up in their beds, a succulent dinner and all the other images of perfection had flown away. Remembering she'd left the frying pan on the stove, she fled to the kitchen, just as the cooking oil burst into flames. The girls screamed, Caitlin stared in horror, and Will quickly grabbed the pan lid, covered the fire and turned off the gas. Caitlin felt like bursting into tears. An unpleasant smell penetrated the kitchen. How incompetent she must seem to him!

Jackie and Katy, delighted to see a familiar visitor, were dancing around Will, begging him for a game.

'Sit up at the table. Now.' She served their plates, her sharp tone drawing a look of surprise from Will. Now he would think she was an inadequate aunt, as well. But he merely said quietly, 'I think it's terrific, the way you've stepped in and managed things.'

His kind words only made her more inclined to cry. 'It's all so different from what was supposed to happen.' She could not help her miserable tone of voice.

'In what way different? I have got the right day, haven't I?'

She realized he was looking at the table and wondering why she'd only set places for the girls. He must think she'd intended to serve him sausages and chips in the kitchen. Instead of giving way to tears, she gave a giggle.

'Oh Will, if only you knew how silly I feel!'

He really didn't know what she meant. She had to explain the fiasco that the day had become, when she had wanted so much to impress him. He listened with a smile.

'And I haven't even had a chance to bathe and change,' she finished.

Will turned to the watching girls. 'I want you to eat your tea,' he suggested. 'As soon as you've finished, we're going to have story time, while Caitlin makes herself pretty, okay?'

He gave Caitlin a gentle push. 'Not another word of self-reproach. Go and take your time. I'll be father tonight. How's that, girls?'

Evidently they approved. Accepting his offer of help, she ran herself a warm bath, splashed in a generous sprinkle of bubble bath and relaxed in the water until her tension evaporated.

Accompanied by the sounds of contented children, she changed into her red dress and did her hair and makeup. By the time she'd finished, Will had both girls settled in bed and was reading them yet another story. He'd even packed up their dishes and restored order to the kitchen. In the dining room, Caitlin quickly covered the sewing table with Heather's best cloth, glassware and the candelabrum. She put the bread in the oven to warm, set out soup bowls and cocktail forks and found a corkscrew for the wine.

Will stared when she came back. 'You look really stunning!'

She knew red suited her, when she had the confidence to wear it.

'You look pretty good yourself,' she reciprocated. As always, his physical presence seemed to sweep aside all the difficulties her mind imagined. Mutual compliments had their effect, changing the family atmosphere to something more intimate, so that she began to tingle as he stood beside her, inspecting the opening course with approval. Caitlin stirred the soup, ladled it out and placed the rolls in a wicker basket, while he opened the wine and lit the candles. Perhaps this meal was going to be successful after all. She was even starting to feel hungry. The table looked just the right setting for a romantic evening to follow.

As she was about to carry the first course to the table, Will came and stood behind her, putting his arms around her and nuzzling the back of her neck. The sensation sent shivers through her but the plates were hot.

'Hey, I'm not on the menu!' She expected him to laugh. Instead, he drew back.

At the table, as she set down his bowl, he said, 'Mind if I ask you a question? Is there something about me you find unattractive?'

The suggestion was so far from the truth that she stared. 'What on earth makes you ask that?'

'At times you're so responsive. Then you seem turned off. I just wondered.'

She felt the blush creep up her cheeks and reach her hairline. The subtle criticism stung. He had no idea of the conflict that kept coming between them, filling her with doubt, dreading his rejection when she told him the truth. Will thought she was moody and cold, when all she longed for was to lie in his arms and throw all caution to the wind. The longer this silence went on, the worse the misunderstandings would become.

Taking a deep breath, she decided to speak out. 'Will, there's something I have to tell you. I've been afraid to.'

Now it was his turn to look surprised. 'You can tell me anything, Caitlin. Surely you know I'm serious about you? I hate secrets.'

'It's difficult.' She took a gulp of wine, uninterested in its quality but hoping it might still the pounding of her heart. Will was looking at her, his deep blue eyes concerned. She simply couldn't speak. An awkward silence followed.

'Pass the salt?' He was trying to deflect the tension that was almost spoiling their interest in the food. She obliged with a small laugh.

In his decisive way, he took control. 'Let's just eat first. You've gone to a lot of trouble to prepare this delicious feast. I intend to do it justice.' He paused, weighing up her response and evidently deciding he was taking the best approach. 'But I warn you, my lady, I'm not going home tonight until I've ferreted out your deep, dark secrets. That is, if I go home at all.'

So he wanted to stay. He'd simply accepted the mishaps and mistakes she'd made tonight. Perhaps he would be as generous when she confessed her past? If so, she knew the desire they'd managed to control would flare into a full expression of their love.

She had no more excuses to avoid telling Will the truth.

7

Course followed course as smoothly as though Caitlin was trained in catering, and her choices had hit the mark with Will. He complimented her several times, and even the silences only confirmed they both relished the food.

Thinking of the disaster he'd walked in to, she smiled across at him.

'Better than sausages and chips?'

'I would have been quite happy with anything you chose to cook for me.'

She felt completely disarmed. Her nerves had settled. Once her story was out in the open, Will would probably dismiss it with a casual wave. Then they could spend the rest of the evening on more satisfying and present concerns.

She was glad she'd gone to so much trouble to dress for him. His expression showed the warm admiration of a man very drawn to a desirable woman. His gaze lingered on her slender neck, the smooth skin of her arms and shoulders, her tiny ears. She imagined him slowly exploring her willing body, until her frustration overflowed in a torrent of response.

The night stretched ahead, enticingly long and private. The girls had kept their promise and hadn't called out even once. Will had already implied he hoped to stay over, and she thought fleetingly how Richard had always watched the clock, hurrying their stolen love to its conclusion so he could be home before his wife's suspicions were aroused. The thought of Richard reminded her of the unpleasant job ahead. No good putting it off. Will was leaning back in his chair, the picture of a well-fed, contented man. The wine bottle was empty and the dishes and leftover scraps packed up on the kitchen bench, waiting to be washed.

Staring across the burned-down candles, Will spoke in an encouraging way. 'Well, are you going to make me wait until breakfast, or share whatever's on your mind now?'

She had rehearsed this speech a hundred times, intending to go into lengthy explanations about how her affair had begun. She and Richard had both been interested in amateur dramatics, and had met at the local club when auditions were offered for a coming production. Both were given small parts. As a result, they met regularly at rehearsals over a period of months. Sometimes Richard picked her up as he lived just a few streets from her address.

He'd begun sharing the problems his marriage was going through. He said his wife showed no interest in any of his hobbies and called his play-acting 'just another of his fantasies'. Caitlin remembered feeling sorry for him when he told her that. Apparently Richard had married an unimaginative woman who knew nothing of dreams beyond the sensible realms of family, career success and a well-planned retirement. She recalled his air of wistful hope. *Caitlin? Do you understand? Can a man want more than his life offers?* Suddenly he'd turned to her and held her tightly, as though he couldn't bear the thought she might slip from his grasp.

'Caitlin?'

She gave a start. Will was waiting patiently for her to begin, when she was already halfway through the tale. It had ended, of course, as all affairs sooner or later had to end. Reminded of that pain, and wanting to be done with the memories, she said in a rush, 'Will, I had a love affair a year ago with a married man.'

She hadn't meant to put it quite so bluntly. At least it was out. Already she felt relieved. Will had only to show her it had nothing to do with their present, and she would never need to think of Richard again. Coming out of her reverie, she raised her eyes to look at him. His expression was hard to fathom. He seemed to be looking at her as though seeing her for the first time.

'You found that out later?'

A jolt of intuition pulled her into the present. It wasn't going to be the simple matter she'd hoped for. She had no intention of lying.

'I knew he was married before anything happened.'

He was silent. She did nothing to break the tension creasing his forehead and giving him a brooding look of doubt.

'At least there were no children involved?'

She began to feel hostile to his questioning. If he had some system of demerit points in relation to extramarital affairs, she did not want to know her score.

'Richard had three children. His wife worked in an insurance office. They always went north and camped at Christmas time. What else would you like to know?'

Will ignored her defensive words. 'I see. You and Richard sat around discussing his domestic life before you went to bed together. And I expect you cooked him little candlelit dinners too?'

Furious, she blushed. One of her daydreams had been Richard coming to dinner at her place. Only once had that ever happened. His visits were always late, when he told his wife he had to attend a Rotary meeting. Will's sarcasm might be fed by jealousy, yet he was directly reminding her of the guilt she'd often felt, knowing Richard's lies maintained two lives. Unlike her, he'd had domestic security as well as a hidden world of desire and deception.

Suddenly she was angry. Why was it that men cast you in a certain role? To Richard she'd been nothing but a mistress — alluring, sexy, available and undemanding. Never could she show him the side that was domestic. He'd never seen her through a bout of flu or helped clear up after a late dinner-party. She could never talk about her desire to one day have children and a home of her own.

Whereas Will had decided she was

sweet, innocent and free from all the conflict and contradictions a real person displayed. Admitting her past made her a human being who'd made mistakes and desired a man apart from himself.

'How dare you judge me! You have no idea what the circumstances were.'

Shielded by her flaring anger, she no longer cared that he thought her calculating and selfish.

'It's hard to imagine any circumstances that could persuade you it was right to climb into another woman's marriage bed.'

His harsh tone might be his own defense against the hurt his wife had dealt him. No! She dismissed that excuse. He should have dealt with his emotions long ago.

She faced him defiantly. 'Have you asked yourself why you think anyone who has an affair is evil?'

'People who betray trust don't deserve my forgiveness.'

'They do!' she insisted. How cold

and defensive he was! 'Everybody deserves forgiveness if they've made an honest mistake.'

'An honest mistake? Come on, Caitlin, who are you deluding?'

He was pacing as though trying to outstrip his anger.

'It's only yourself you're hurting, Will.'

'What's that supposed to mean?' He swung and faced her, his glare gimlet-sharp.

'You've gone on brooding over your wife's failings far too long. Who do you think is suffering? I doubt Patricia even thinks of you. It's too long ago. And she would have had her reasons for her behavior. Maybe she thought you didn't love her.'

Apparently she'd said the unforgivable. His look of fury changed to a mask of detachment.

'A psychologist, as well as an easy lay?'

His arrogance was outrageous. She felt the warm flush drain from her face. Driven by a primitive urge, she stepped forward to slap his face but he caught her by the wrist and pulled her toward him. Suddenly he was running his finger seductively down the length of her bare throat. His gesture did not convey the slightest affection, yet was so sensual she had to fight her impulse to let her head fall back and allow his persuasive hands to fondle the throbbing flesh above her heart. He was treating her as available — as he'd said, *an easy lay*.

Now desire and anger inflamed them both, to the point where she felt inclined to prove him right. Let him look down on her! He was like so many men who were quick to enjoy a night's pleasure before they walked away in contempt. Her self-esteem was shattered. She could forget her ideas of love and romance. The women who'd laughed at her ideals were right.

Caitlin looked back at Will objectively. Any feelings of love for him were frozen now. She saw a tall, good-looking man in his prime — an available man who, at her signal, would pick her up and carry her to the bed, rip off her dress and use her with all the sensuality and skill he was surely capable of. She could close her eyes, forget her ideals and sink into her rising passions. A flash of clear insight warned her that to sleep with Will when they were further apart than ever would be wrong. Thrills and excitement might be set loose by their angry passion, but they would only despise each other, come the morning. No, she must turn him down. He was too fixed in his opinions and too sure about the way the world should be.

He was still caressing her. His knowing fingers slid over her shoulders, lightly touched her throat, and teased the shadowed cleft of her breasts. He was deliberately playing with her, allowing her want to build. Staring at the guttering candles, she felt paralyzed; letting him work on her physical response even as she reminded herself she must put a stop to this before it was too late.

As though from a far distance, she heard knocking. Slowly she registered that someone was at the door. Tony and Heather's friends dropped by at the weirdest times.

'Expecting anyone?'

'Of course not. Send them away,' she murmured. Unless she and Will resolved this tension, he would probably walk out of her life forever. All the evening had so far generated for them both was doubt, disappointment and sexual frustration. Not a recipe for a happy future! Will would decide she wasn't worth the trouble. And she had to know if he'd really meant those cruel words. It was possible he'd merely been reacting to unbearably painful memories.

Will went abruptly to the door, his step impatient. Clearly he hadn't welcomed the intrusion any more than she had. He must have known he'd had her literally in the palm of his hand. She'd been on the point of surrender, regardless of consequences. At least she could try and compose herself before he came back. Still dizzy with arousal, she filled a glass with cold water, then pressed her hands to her burning cheeks. She heard his step in the hall. He'd certainly wasted no time. She turned to face him.

Martin stood there, an uncertain smile on his face and a bunch of drooping flowers in his hand. He thrust them at her awkwardly. Caitlin stared at him.

'Exactly what do you want?' Her tone was icy. 'I don't like spontaneous visits, particularly when I'm in the middle of a private evening with a friend.' She looked past Martin. 'Where's Will?'

Martin sounded highly embarrassed as he stood there, changing the flowers from hand to hand. 'Gee, I'm sorry,' he murmured. 'Will went home.'

'Went home?'

'He looked at me, then the flowers. He said, 'What do you want?' So I told him I'd come to talk to you about our secret. He seemed kind of funny. Oh yes, he said, 'Tell Caitlin thanks, and you're next in the queue.' I guess he thought . . .'

She did not have to work overtime to visualize the scene on the doorstep. Furious that Will would make such a cutting remark to Martin, whom she hardly knew, she glared at him.

'What a ridiculous assumption!' she began, then, remembering the series of impromptu visits and the flowers, she fixed her unwanted visitor with a stern look. 'Martin, Will and I have a serious relationship. I don't have the slightest interest in any other man, including you. I hope that's clear?'

'Of course! I bought the flowers for Angela. You said I ought to be direct with her and I went to ask her to be my partner at the masked ball. She wasn't home. I just felt disappointed and then I thought of you, all by yourself.' He dropped the bunch on the table. 'I thought, well, Caitlin might like these, otherwise they'll only die.'

He sounded so abject she almost

reached out to ruffle his hair. 'Poor Martin! Seems like neither of us has a successful love life at present.'

'I did want to see what happened to the dog. I shouldn't have said 'our secret' to Will. I thought the girls might overhear. Will got the wrong impression.'

'It doesn't matter.' She felt weary now. The evening had collapsed into farce and she felt worn out. 'The dog's gone.'

'No it hasn't. As soon as I pulled up it ran down the path and tried to get into my car.'

'Oh no! What are we going to do? I suppose we'd better feed it. But if the girls find out, they'll beg to keep it. There'll be an awful scene.'

Martin watched as she began to tip all the leftovers into a mixing bowl.

'Wow! I bet he's never had a meal like that.'

'There's always a first time.' She knew from its scrawny look that the dog must have survived on scraps. Waiting at the gate near Martin's car, the ravenous animal sniffed the air when they carried out the feast.

'Here you go, Charley!' called Martin. They watched as it devoured prawns, chicken and half-eaten buns as though it had stumbled into dog heaven.

'What's with 'Charley'?' Caitlin sounded teasing. 'You're getting attached to him.'

'I once had a dog called Charley. That's all. I'd better go. I'm sorry, Caitlin. What an idiot.'

'We do need to make a decision about the dog. Let's go in and I'll make us a cup of tea.' That was what people did in times of death and disaster.

Inside, she dumped Martin's flowers in a vase of water. Poor things, why leave them to wither, just because the wrong man was in her kitchen and her life was in ruins.

They drank the tea and Martin offered to help wash the dishes. He really was rather sweet. Not many men would be willing to clean up after another man's enjoyment. He was so penitent at having broken up the evening. He needed to make amends, though he couldn't possibly realize the full extent of his ill-timed visit.

She was still stunned by Will's harshness toward her. All very well for Heather to point out no man was perfect, but what right had Will to label Caitlin as faultless, then despise her when she admitted she was only a human being with many facets to her nature? Better he'd gone home, rather than the alternative they'd been headed for. Sex was a powerful force, sometimes just as much for harm as good. Probably he would have discarded her like a used theatre ticket. There'd been too much anger, too much conflict.

'I'd better go.'

Martin had dried the last of the dishes, all the while talking about Angela until at last Caitlin asked, 'What makes you think Angela is interested in you?'

She was surprised when he said,

'Because she said so. Well, in a way. Her words were 'I'm a girl who likes good times. I'm not ready to be serious, but when I am you'll be the first to know.' So she must like me.'

'Yes. It sounds as though she must.' Perhaps Angela, like other people she could name, was afraid of making an exclusive commitment.

'So you don't think I'm an idiot?'

'Of course not.' She was the last person to laugh at the heart's impulses. 'But maybe she means exactly what she says. She may not want a steady boyfriend.'

'I can wait.'

'Oh, Martin!' His chivalrous attitude touched her. He sounded like a knight determined to win his lady, regardless of obstacles. To Caitlin, he seemed very young, and yet she needed to hear his determined faith tonight, when Will had apparently walked out of her life. She felt a flicker of hope. Perhaps even now some miracle would put things right.

'Just tell me and I'll go home.'

Even Martin's company felt better than nothing.

'It's all right. It doesn't matter if you want to stay. Maybe there's something on TV, or we could have a game of cards.' She didn't fancy a solitary evening mulling over the hard words that had been exchanged. She found the cribbage board and taught him the rudiments of the game, then suggested coffee.

'Would you rather I stayed away until Tony gets back?'

'No. Jackie and Katy are pleased to see you. Just let me know in advance if you're coming.'

'If you like, we could take the girls to the zoo tomorrow. Have you been?'

She hadn't, and was interested to compare the facilities with Auckland's zoo.

'I think I'll accept your offer. We're both at a loose end. It's better than brooding.'

And besides, there was the issue of the homeless dog. Something would have to be done.

'I think you're a very sensible person,' Martin said, his tone respectful. 'I've never had an older woman as a friend before.'

She had to laugh. 'When you've lived as long as I have, you become wise.'

Outside, the dog was nowhere to be seen. At least she could defer that problem until tomorrow. She waved goodnight, thinking what a contrast Martin's old car was to Will's Porsche. Would she ever ride in it again? He would stay away as long as he believed tonight's fiasco. So he thought she was easy game? He might be skilled at arousing her desire, but he had a lot to learn about her. His condescending manner was enough to make her furious. No wonder his wife had run off the rails if he'd treated her in the same way.

Martin tooted and drove away. Even if he spoke to her as though she had wrinkles and grey hair, she liked him. His sincerity and lack of cynicism touched her, and in a certain way she was flattered that he treated her as a fount of wisdom. If only he knew the truth!

Before she went to bed, she arranged the abandoned flowers in a second vase. They hadn't the glamour of Will's roses, but reflected Martin's choice of humble garden blooms, somehow as innocent as the young man himself. She set them on the kitchen table and carried the roses to her bedroom. She would see them as soon as she opened her eyes in the morning; all she had to remind her that, against the odds, love might bloom.

* * *

In the accepting way of children, Jackie and Katy had settled down to having Caitlin as their temporary mother. After the chaos of the first few days, they found their aunt was a kind but firm parent who often thought up surprises and treats for them, yet could be as strict as Heather if they misbehaved.

She was enjoying her crash course in child care. Their amusing sayings and fresh perceptions were entertaining. Their endless needs kept her busy, giving her less time to brood over her last exchange with Will. He made no attempt to contact her. Although she was tempted, she resisted the urge to call him. He thought she was a home-wrecker and his failure to understand the illogical urges of emotion was hard to forgive. Surely he too had followed his heart down alleys and by-ways, sometimes loving the wrong person? His clutching at the past was surely just as negative as any attachment he accused her of. As long as he refused to discuss these issues, she did not intend to chase after him. Hard as it might be to accept, perhaps they were wrong for each other.

She was grateful for Martin's uncomplicated company over the next days. As promised, he took them all to Taronga Park zoo. It was an exhausting day, with two children wilting in the heat yet demanding to see the never-ending varieties of native animals, birds, reptiles and exotic species. Gone were the sad days when wild creatures were locked in small cages under the prying eyes of strangers. The zoo attempted to create spacious natural habitats, and had a number of breeding programs in connection with endangered species protection. As the girls ran from one vantage point to the next, Caitlin turned to Martin.

'I would never have managed this alone. Thank you.'

'I think they're enjoying themselves.'

'You seem good with children, Martin.'

He looked pleased at the compliment. 'There were six kids in my family. Mum went out to work, so I learned to muck in and help.'

Was that why he gravitated to Caitlin? Perhaps he could shed responsibility and simply be a younger brother, while she in turn gave him sisterly advice. Her mind flashed back to Will's assumption that the young man was having an affair with her, and she almost laughed aloud. A platonic friendship was so much easier.

Allowing the girls to run along the fenced lake edge where water birds fished, dived or strutted on the banks, they sat companionably, watching. Without sexual involvement or emotional needs, people behaved in an entirely different way. There were no sudden flaring jealousies or misunderstandings. Love flourished in a different climate from friendship, which was obvious. She wouldn't mind a bit when Martin moved out of her life, whereas the thought of leaving Will caused her actual heartache.

Martin wasn't immune from love's pangs either. He was still determined to escort Angela to the masked ball. Caitlin privately doubted the girl deserved such faithful devotion. He was convinced his romantic dreams were about to come true. Caitlin lay back on the grass, half-listening and wishing that Will was here with her. How strange it was. An onlooker would assume they were a family, yet each was far away, lost in a private world of hopes and disappointments.

They walked on, reaching a kiosk where cold drinks and snacks revived their flagging energies. Martin was a generous escort. He insisted they should each take home a memento of the day. The girls chose toy koalas, Martin bought a T-shirt, and Caitlin chose a set of table mats adorned with Australian wildflowers. They would remind her of this holiday when she was back in her old routine of hospital work and her isolated time off. How well would she cope with that, after the activity and noise she'd grown used to here?

'Ready to head home?' Martin had settled the bill and the girls had wilted. Clearly they'd had enough for one day. Swinging drowsy Katy up in his arms and handing Jackie an ice block, he led the way toward the exit.

As Martin dropped them at their gate, Caitlin was relieved the homeless dog was nowhere in sight. Perhaps it went off to forage during the day. She felt desperately sorry for the poor creature. Dog shelters were notoriously overcrowded during the holiday season, and the skinny, nervous animal would be unlikely to find a new home. However, soon she would have no other option, except to contact the ranger.

If only she could talk over the problem with Will and ask his advice! But she had to face the possibility that their rift was permanent. She certainly wouldn't contact him first.

She was sitting a few days later, half-watching a quiz program, when the phone rang. Heather usually called about this time to check up on her family. Expecting to hear her sister, Caitlin panicked when Will's strong voice registered.

'I've been thinking over what you said.' He made no excuses for his silence.

'Oh?' What exactly had she said? The evening was a haze of unfortunate memories. Was he referring to her confession? If so, she'd decided it was none of his business. She had no more to say about a liaison long gone from her life.

'I agree with you.' He assumed she understood him. Obviously he'd spent their separation mulling over their evening, too.

'You agree?'

'I've held on far too long.'

'Held on?' She was starting to feel like the bird at the picnic ground, repeating whatever his audience said. Will seemed to be on automatic pilot, following his line of thought to its conclusion.

'So I'm doing something about it.'

She waited patiently for him to come to the point.

'Yes. I'm going to Melbourne next weekend.'

'Permanently?' Despite herself, disappointment must have echoed in her voice, and he replied, sounding puzzled, 'No, of course not.'

Her relief almost masked his next words. He was saying something about business. Had he ever mentioned business interests in Melbourne? And why bother to ring her, just to inform her he was going away?

'Well, have a nice time.' She made herself sound offhand, not wanting him to know her feelings. His words simply confirmed what she already knew. If he preferred to make a trip interstate to attend to some financial deal, when she only had a few more weeks in Australia, he evidently cared even less than she'd hoped.

'I want you to have dinner with me before I go.' He sounded determined.

'You've forgotten I'm babysitting.'

'The girls can come too.'

She could think of several reasons to turn him down and was about to enumerate them when he spoke again.

'It's absolutely necessary you come. We had a complete misunderstanding the other night. Shall we say tomorrow?'

'Martin's stopping by tomorrow.' She'd promised to patch his jeans as a return favor for his help. If Will intended to throw another jealous scene she would tell him her spare time was her own, to spend with whom she pleased. Possessiveness was no substitute for love.

But he merely said quietly, 'In that case, Thursday? I'll pick you up at five o'clock.'

She agreed to go. Even the pleasing timbre of his voice had set up an ache to see him again.

After the phone call, she sat for a long time, staring into space as though gathering her strength. Their next meeting would decide their future, one way or the other.

8

As the time of the dinner date approached, she began to feel as she used to at the amateur dramatics club: waiting in the wings, convinced she would forget her lines and make a fool of herself. The girls refused to sit patiently. Even before they left home their clothes looked ready for the wash. Caitlin had changed her outfit three times. She'd pinned up her auburn hair, then brushed it and left it loose. She'd used a musky perfume, then scrubbed it off and substituted a floral toilet water. She'd changed from sandals to high heels, then back to sandals.

The girls thought all this was great fun. They wanted to do the same and were in the midst of an argument about party frocks when Will pulled up in an old kombi van she hadn't seen before.

It must be the work vehicle he used for carrying hardware.

'Where's the fancy car?' She grinned, knowing his pride in his Porsche.

Will returned her smile and it was hard to remember they'd had such an intense disagreement just a few days before.

'I thought we'd go to the beach and have a quick swim on the way.'

'Why not?' It was a lovely afternoon, sunny and still warm. Jackie and Katy would settle all the easier after a swim. And it would solve the party frock issue.

'I'll just run in and pick up bathers and towels.'

Will went to wait by the van while Caitlin organized the girls. So much for all her fuss over hair and makeup. A few minutes in the surf would quickly restore the natural look.

But the idea of a swim appealed. Until Jackie and Katy had eaten and settled quietly, no serious talk would be possible. The children's interruptions made sane conversation impossible and she had to wonder how Heather and Tony ever managed to discuss their private life at all. Perhaps married couples became swamped by their families and had to forget they were individuals.

She could hear some altercation outside. She called the girls and ran out to the gate, in time to see the dog flee from next door, pursued by an ugly-looking fellow brandishing a broom and a sack. Shouting obscenities, he came to a stop when Will stepped forward, the animal cowering behind his legs.

'What seems to be the trouble?'

His words were polite but his presence was powerful. His air of authority confirmed why he'd been allotted the role of Prince of Lochac. The man, who appeared to be drunk, broke into a tirade of rage.

'I'll teach that mongrel not to run away.' He waved the broom about in a threatening way until Will simply took hold of the handle and levered it from his grasp. Eyeing the terrified dog, he stepped closer to the drunk.

'And you'll tie him in that sack? And then what? Drop him in the creek?'

By now the dog was trying to make itself invisible behind Will's shoes.

Signaling the girls to stay behind her, Caitlin added her explanation. 'They abandoned the dog. Just moved out and left it, nearly a week ago.'

The man made an aggressive move toward her but Will was quicker, seizing him in a powerful grip. Assuming the attacking stance of a swordsman, he looked ready to run the fellow through with the broom.

'Are you threatening my lady?' Even his language had reverted. 'You're a bully. Get lost.' With a shove, he set the fellow free to stumble away, still muttering his ugly words.

'That was impressive.' Caitlin was surprised to feel her legs shaking. She hated physical violence, and if Will hadn't stepped in, she dreaded the fate of the poor shivering animal, now being consoled by the girls. Caitlin briefly explained how the situation had come about.

'What do I do now?' What if the drunk hung about until they drove away, then captured the dog and sealed its fate?

Will was thinking. 'Easily fixed. Here boy.' Opening the kombi door, he gestured, and with a willing spring the dog jumped in. 'We'll take him with us. He might like a run on the sand, and I know a dog-friendly beach not far from here.'

She could have cried with relief. With his support, they would figure out the problem together. And she realized that was just another facet of love — two people working hand in hand to help and support each other.

It was a busy time, with early home-bound traffic congesting the roads. In the rear of the van, the girls sang tunelessly, while the enraptured dog sat watching the passing scenery with an air of quaint supervision. Caitlin registered Will's presence beside her like an electrical current. The connection she felt was truer than words, which could hurt or mislead.

When Will pulled up, she thought the beach seemed vaguely familiar, though she'd only been swimming in Australia at the local pool. The glassy breakers alarmed her. She wasn't used to surf and wondered if it was safe to confront the surging rollers that smashed the shore with such a thunderous sound. Fortunately for the girls, there was a kind of placid salt lake, formed where the tide ran in and filled a hollow of the beach. Children were safe there. It was only knee-deep and plenty of watchful parents lined its banks. Meanwhile, Will allowed the dog free rein to explore. Clearly the animal had never seen sand or ocean, and appeared intoxicated by the scents. He wasn't willing to go near the water, and when Will picked up a few sticks to toss, the animal retreated, clearly expecting to be hurt.

Will sat down. 'Come here, boy,' he invited, turning to Caitlin. 'What's his name?'

'I don't think he has one.' The epithets she'd heard shouted at him were hardly suitable. 'I think Martin calls him Charley.'

'Charley's as good a name as any.' The dog had crept closer and was accepting Will's fondling, though he shivered from time to time, as though only associating touch with pain.

'I'll get the girls changed,' Caitlin said, leaving them to make friends.

By the time she returned, the dog was sniffing among the heaps of seaweed, driftwood and the occasional fish carcass washed up by the sea. Will stood by the lagoon, his black bathers setting off his narrow hips and muscular thighs as he chatted to a woman who was watching her children play in the water. With cries of pleasure, Jackie and Katy raced into the warm pool.

'Caitlin, meet my neighbor, Wendy. She's offered to supervise the girls while you take a dip in the surf with me.'

'You go and enjoy a proper swim,' Wendy confirmed. 'I promise not to take my eyes off your girls.'

There was little option and Caitlin followed reluctantly as Will headed down the beach. The look of the menacing waves slowed her pace, but pride compelled her to keep going. Perhaps Australians took such seas for granted, but she'd grown up on gentler shores. Taking a deep breath and crossing her fingers for luck, she saw a translucent green wall tower up ahead, and race toward her. She dived for dear life. To her surprise, the rushing tide exhilarated her. She broke the surface, all in one piece, and turned to face the next onslaught.

Will, who was well ahead, seemed suddenly to disappear. She could not scan the swimmers thoroughly, with the never-ceasing breakers towering above, but minutes seemed to pass. His sleek black head was nowhere to be seen. She began to worry. Even experts might come to grief in such conditions. Could anything have happened to him?

Adults and young people forged on to deeper water or waited, poised to catch a wave and body-surf in to shore. No one looked at her. What should one do in an emergency? Make some signal for those Herculean young lifesavers to hurtle from the club house, dash to the water and embark on a rescue mission? Where *was* Will? Panicky, she missed an oncoming dumper and was picked up, whirled around like an insect in a hurricane and painfully dragged along the last few meters of gritty sand. The offending wave dissolved and trickled back to her as innocent foam. She felt a complete fool as she shook salt water from her face and hair and opened her eyes to see Will laughing at her.

'Poor water rat! I should have stayed with you. I forgot you're not used to our surf.'

'Where were you?' She mustered up

her dignity, not admitting how concerned she'd been on his behalf.

'You weren't worried about me?' He sounded amused and she shook her head.

'Of course not!'

But he saw she'd had a fright and offered his hand as they waded back to face the breakers.

'It's better further out. The water's calmer where it's deep. You *can* swim?'

To show him she wasn't a complete idiot she submerged and caught his legs, tugging until he collapsed. He joined in a tussle until they were forced apart as water eddied wildly around them. She clutched him again, this time to stop herself undergoing another unwanted ride to shore. There was something stimulating about this confrontation with the ocean, which had the power to sweep her away and even annihilate her. No time for hesitation or fear — one simply had to exert one's own puny strength, discovering the limits of the body, learning to flow with the mighty forces. It was a symbol of life itself with its struggles, falls and occasional moments of uplifting joy.

The feel of his body close to hers gave her security in this watery world. He was solid and reliable. Again she went under and held fast to his legs, laughing as they both surfaced. Will pinned her arms firmly, embracing her.

'You'd like to drown me?'

She couldn't stop laughing, until she swallowed a mouthful of salt water.

'This is such fun!' If only they could stay like this, with nothing to interfere, nothing to confuse or threaten them. Just the sea, the sun, the blue sky and surrender as Will's arms embraced her . . .

A riderless surfboard careered past, narrowly missing them, its owner in pursuit after a mistimed wave had sent him flying. She'd never tried the sport, and asked, 'Do you surf?'

Will nodded. 'Most boys here learn, and girls too, these days. In my teens, girls mainly came to the beach to watch us.'

She could imagine adolescent beach parties with teenagers checking out one another, just as young men and women had created rituals to meet and mate in every country and century of the world's history. Nothing important would have changed. As the day faded, food and drink would be provided. Later, under the stars, couples would find quiet nooks and crannies to explore the erotic impulses that showed them they had left childhood forever.

Suddenly she realized why the beach seemed familiar.

'Is this where we came, the first time?'

'Yes. Close to home, weren't we?'

She remembered every detail of that moonlit night — the sound of barely-visible rollers breaking on the sand and the surge of their own passion. Will had controlled his desire, while admitting its strength. *You really are an attractive girl. I don't think I could take responsibility if we spend the next hours together like this. And we have plenty of time.*

Well, words to that effect . . . but not only words. As for having plenty of time, how much more of the brief span left would they waste on fights, misunderstandings, or all the other excuses that prevented them from admitting they were in love?

Her resolve grew firm. Tonight there would be no escape from the truth. She would tell Will her true feelings for him and risk whatever that brought. She turned and let a huge cresting wave sweep her on a breathtaking ride back to shore. As they waded from the surf, they were greeted by a rapturous dog, running back and forth just beyond the waterline. Already his timid manner was lifting. His tail wagged cautiously as Will called him.

'Hey Charley, come here, boy.'

'He seems to like you,' Caitlin observed, as the dog followed close on their heels.

Wendy stood up when she saw them, and beckoned her own offspring. 'I think they've had a good time.' She pointed out the castle and moat standing on the bank of the lagoon.

Will thanked her and she smiled in an open way that told Caitlin his good looks had not gone unnoticed. 'Pleased to help,' she said. 'Just let me know, any time you need a sitter.'

Obviously she must think he was an uncle to the girls.

'How did you two become friends?'

Will looked surprised at Caitlin's question. 'She lives a few doors down the road from me. I helped her a couple of times, when her house sprang leaks after the storms. We're not exactly friends.'

'She seemed pretty friendly.'

She said no more when his shrug suggested otherwise. Will clearly had no idea of his effect on women. He settled back to wait while the girls finished their building project, and she joined him, thinking about domestic life. In spite of its demands, there was a calm, fulfilling pleasure in helping in a child's growth. Perhaps Will had similar thoughts. His expression was satisfied, and his gaze settled on a pregnant young woman, who lay sunbathing in the balmy warmth of late afternoon. She was unselfconscious in a two-piece outfit that revealed a nut-brown mound. In just a few months, she would have a living child. Exchanging one's single life for parenthood must be an enormous step. Yet, with Will, the prospect was suddenly appealing.

Beside them, the dog sat observing as seagulls flew past in a squawking crowd. Unable to resist temptation, he dashed after them, barking loudly. He looked like any other happy animal enjoying playtime at the beach.

'I can't believe it's the same creature.' There was a lump in Caitlin's throat as she explained the whole story, sensing Will's anger at the poor dog's ill-treatment. 'I'm so worried!' she went on. 'If I take him home, that awful man might come back. Heather won't have him, and if he goes to the pound, I doubt he'll find a home. He's not a pedigree or a cute pup.'

'Just an ordinary bitser, that's for sure.' Will took her hand. 'How about he stays with me?'

'Really?' Her heart filled with gratitude. 'Do you want a dog?'

'Why not? He's a good-natured fellow.'

'But what about your travels?'

'Here, stop worrying!' He smiled down at her and she felt her heart throb with emotion. 'He'll be my responsibility, not yours. I promise you he won't be ignored or ill-treated. If I have to be away, I'll arrange for his proper care.'

'Oh Will, I love you!'

Caitlin bit her lip. The unguarded words had slipped out. His face wore a look of hope, but he just dropped a soft kiss on her cheek.

'Come on!' He offered a hand and pulled her to her feet. 'Let's get the troops on board and head home to my place.'

She was relieved the girls had enjoyed a tiring hour swimming and running in the fresh air. She did not want two wide-awake owls to interfere with the discussion that lay ahead. They were starting to wilt now, ploughing up the dunes toward the kombi van. How well she remembered those dunes, and the jetty further down the beach where she'd first admitted her attraction to the tall man by her side. Shouldering beach towels and bags, he strode ahead, his tanned physique attracting the glances of other women. Regardless of his surroundings, he adapted easily. Whether in swimmers, casual dress or the garb of a prince, his appearance was striking. Tossing her damp hair and adjusting her posture to best advantage, she hurried to catch up, hoping onlookers would see them as a well-matched couple.

Frank words would be exchanged if their meeting was to have any real point. Jackie and Katy defused the atmosphere as their questions and demands for food, drink, and attention occupied Caitlin. Will encouraged the girls to feed the dog with kibble biscuits purchased on the ride home, then Caitlin bathed the children while Will made dinner. By the time the meal was over, they were yawning and rubbing their eyes. When they were told it was bedtime, they trotted off to the old fold-down sofa in Will's spare room, and did not even want a bedtime story.

The silence was a strange contrast. Curled up asleep, the warm, satisfied dog had found itself a comfortable spot on the old rug Will had thrown down.

'Coffee? It's freshly brewed.'

'You're a magician.'

She felt languorous. After the wine, the sun and the swim, relaxation seeped through her as she rested back on the comfortable couch and wondered why she'd ever thought it would be hard to talk to Will. Together at last! He set down the cups to cool, sat beside her, and placed a warm arm around her shoulders. She nestled against him.

'I really overreacted the other night,' he said. 'I owe you an apology.'

Remembering his harsh words, she was silent.

'I wouldn't blame you, if you can't forgive me.'

She saw he was genuine, and was able to set aside those hurtful accusations. It seemed he'd decided that her past, and his own, should not matter now. She was glad she'd been honest at the risk of losing him. The fact was that she was here, and his embrace enfolded her as though he never wanted her to leave. Surely that proved he cared for her as a real person, virtues, faults and all. She was free of pretense and he could love her as she was.

The soft music cast its peaceful spell over the fading light of evening. It was about eight o'clock, for the January days were long. From the window overlooking the sea, lights began to define the curving coast road and little winding hill streets of the suburb. In all those houses, people were settling down to their various evening entertainments. The privilege of being alone with Will, with no unwanted phone calls or uninvited visitors, filled her with anticipation. He'd already indicated he felt the same, for he'd switched off his cell phone.

'Not expecting important calls?' she teased.

'The only matter of importance tonight is our future.'

Her pulse throbbed at his determined tone. He had come to the same point she'd reached. It was time to stop holding back, time to deal with the last unanswered questions.

'I want to ask you one thing, Will. Why do you have to go to Melbourne so suddenly? I'm disappointed. There's so little time before I leave Australia.'

'And that's exactly why I have to go now.'

'You mentioned business?'

'Unfinished business, actually. You

were quite right, Caitlin. I do have to see Patricia.'

So that explained 'Pattie', the lovely young girl in the photograph still on display in his kitchen. Enshrining her image as she must have looked when they first met as teenagers seemed a strangely possessive action.

She wanted to understand. Yes, he ought to visit his ex-wife and realize she too was probably a woman he had idealized. He remembered her as self-willed and immature, but she too had surely learned from youthful mistakes. Will would discover she was just an ordinary woman making her way through life like everyone else.

'I think you're doing the right thing.'

'I have to. I'm risking too much, expecting you to live with my past when I hadn't the sense to see you were shedding yours.'

'My feelings for Richard faded some time ago.' She was pleased to make that statement. Yearning for the past was a sad waste of time, when right in front of her was a new life, waiting to be accepted with grateful hands.

'I suppose you'd never have told me about him, if you were still involved.'

'That's right. Now I'm ready for the real deal, as you Australians say.' She laughed at the turn of phrase. It was true. She didn't want half measures and unavailable men. She didn't want a compartmented life.

'The whole bit, eh?' Dropping the slang, he drew her closer. 'In that case I have something for you.'

He began to caress her until she felt her last resistance evaporate. If his hands had lacked tenderness the last time he'd touched her in this way, he was making up for that now.

'Caitlin, I've wanted to make love to you from the very first time I saw you. I can't get you out of my mind. It's not just desire. I want to know you and share my life with you . . . '

So this was the moment her life had been leading her to, when the man destiny had chosen for her offered her his troth. In an intuitive flash she saw their future together. Never to be alone again, to share a common purpose, while continuing to grow and develop as individuals. Will's persuasive kisses stopped her overactive mind and she allowed herself to respond, showing him with her lips and hands and yielding body that she was ready to belong to him.

He stood up. Gathering her in his arms, he carried her to his bedroom and laid her down gently on the quilt.

'Wait there, my darling. I'm going to lock up. No one's going to disturb us tonight. Time's too short.'

She nodded. Before the night was over, she knew he would ask her to marry him. She would accept, they would be lovers, a whole lifetime welcomed them as a couple willing to take the risks of loving again. They would wave goodbye to all the lessons of the past. A sense of joy and freedom overwhelmed her and her heart throbbed with happiness.

While she waited, she recognized a familiar object on the bedside table. Of course she'd known all along that he'd purchased that bracelet for her, the day they'd gone to the Central Coast. It must be what he was referring to, when he'd said he had something to give her. He'd probably had some romantic words inscribed, just for her. She was sure that, when she read them, they would make the whole night's promise come true.

Lifting the lid of the velvet-covered box, she decided a quick peep would not be too dishonorable. Yes! The bracelet nestled in its blue silk lining and the inscription plate, which had been blank, was engraved in tiny, ornate lettering. She bent closer to make out the words.

As she read *To My Beautiful Pattie*, a sense of terrible misunderstanding replaced Caitlin's thoughts of her future with Will. It wasn't herself, after all, who had the power to win his love. His designs on her must be of quite another kind. And she'd only found out by accident. What an actor he was! Once again, her romantic nature had swept her to the brink of heartbreak.

Unable to believe she was so wrong in her assessment of Will, she took the bracelet from its case; as though hoping the words she'd read were a hallucination she'd concocted to counter her intense happiness. Again she faced the inscription. *My Beautiful Pattie* . . . those words sealed the end of her illusion. Will had no intention of ever letting go of his ex-wife. She might have changed, even remarried, yet in Will's mind Patricia belonged to him. Her presence would prevent any other woman from ever reaching him.

The guard he must have posted around his heart was so powerful that apparently he could do anything, say anything, never really meaning a word of it. Like a skillful actor on stage, he could assume the mantle of romantic lover, debonair man of the world or successful business man, while all along the roles were no more to him than a series of costumes he could don and discard as he pleased. The women he must have hurt along the way were left to puzzle over promises they thought he'd made with every appearance of sincerity. Martin's Angela and her peculiar phone call now made sense. The poor girl must have taken Will's play-acting seriously, imagining he was genuine. Heather, too, had entertained false impressions about Will. And she'd been absolutely right, for the pain now coursing through Caitlin was every bit as acute as her recent joy. She could not even begin to find words to describe Will's nature.

A chill crept through her body as she sat on the edge of the bed, re-buttoning her shirt with shaking hands. Betrayed trust was one of the worst pains. No wonder so many wounded lovers decided to turn off their emotions, and never risk loving again. That way you were safe. To expose yourself to this kind of hurt was madness. The future she'd dreamed of with Will now seemed like a cruel delusion. Had they ever gone as far as a permanent relationship, the reality would have been doubt and constant reminders she was only second-best. At their most intimate moments, she would have been wondering if his thoughts were far away with a lost love. The humiliation made her shiver.

She could hear him coming back, his step confident. So he thought he'd done the job well, primed her ready for the kill? He knew he had access to her feelings and would have no compunction about taking his opportunity. She was only a visitor. In a week or two she'd be gone, a pleasant, passing interlude without demands or upsets to his smoothly-running existence. He had his home, his Porsche, his building plans, his social life. And of course his memories. What else did a man need, apart from an occasional fling with an agreeable woman?

Caitlin did not look at him as he

entered the room. He went to the dressing table, opened a small drawer and took something out. Paralyzed, she sensed him walk to her, sit beside her, take her small hand and press a jewelry box in her hand.

'This is for you,' he said lovingly. 'I think you know why.'

Like a robot, she opened the hinged top and saw the ring she had tried on at the antique shop counter. She felt she was in a dreadful dream. Reality had deserted her. She could believe nothing her senses conveyed. Will's gentle voice, his tender touch and his words, were all delusions. What she had interpreted as love had turned out to be lies. Her anticipation of marriage had changed to a quick and cheap holiday affair. She'd thought Will was strong, caring, directed, desirable. He was nothing but a coward, hiding behind past failure, too afraid to risk real love.

Her eyes smarting with tears, she turned to meet his waiting gaze. How could she bear that false romanticism in his look? He'd perfected the expression of a suitor longing to hear words of acceptance from his lady love.

'Caitlin? Will you marry me?' He moved to take her in his arms. Her rage erupted at his falseness.

'I loathe you, Will. I'd never marry you! I hope after tonight I never see you or hear your name again.' Unable to bear her disappointment, she hurled the ring box across the room. It struck the wall and rolled away with a dull thud. Shaking with fury, she stared at him as though trying to see past his mask to the real, deceitful man within.

His face had frozen in a look of uncomprehending shock. She saw the rigidity of his body as he slowly stood and walked across the room. He retrieved the ring and replaced it in its container. He did not have the honesty to concede she'd caught him at his tricks. The fact that she'd exposed his manipulations appeared to make him angry rather than amused.

'I'm surprised to hear that.' He spoke in a voice of freezing calm. 'I had the impression we were about to become lovers. I've just asked you to marry me. I'm sorry, I had no idea I fill you with loathing.'

'You're the most two-faced man I've ever met!'

'And *you* are the most inconsistent woman *I* have ever had the misfortune to care for,' he returned. 'I think it's time we called it a day, don't you, Caitlin?'

Will gave every appearance of struggling with as much hurt and confusion as she felt herself. From across the room he faced her, his frank eyes displaying a stunned expression. He was looking at her warily, as though she might be a little mad.

It was over, she knew. The realization waited for her like an endurance of pain she would have to undergo. At present her outrage at least masked every other feeling. Even so, the hint of the hurt she would have to go through because of this man so coldly facing her, brought a tiny sob from her throat.

'Why did you have to lie to me?' she cried out suddenly.

'I don't understand you.' She could hear the angry dismissal in his voice.

'Stop it! Will, I can see through you. Lies won't work anymore.'

'How dare you call me a liar?' She had broken his self-control. He was as white and infuriated as she was. Let him suffer what he so casually did to other people!

'Are you still pretending you've been honest with me?' Her challenge carried a tone of scorn. She doubted even the most seasoned pretender would try to maintain his façade when confronted like this.

He hesitated. 'I've been relatively honest.'

'*Relatively!*' Sarcasm sharpened her usually gentle voice.

'As far as I'm aware, yes. Apart from one thing, I think I've concealed nothing about myself.'

Far from sounding defensive, he'd reclaimed his aloof manner. In fact he was viewing her as though she was irrational, and certainly unlikeable.

'Has it occurred to you the 'one thing' you've kept to yourself might concern me?'

'As a matter of fact, yes. That's why I've said nothing, so far. Caitlin, why do you think you have the right to hear every fine detail of my life? Do you feel you're entitled to cross-examine me on each personal fact you might feel curious about?'

The best form of defense was attack, apparently. She was ready with her comeback.

'The fact you love Patricia still, while proposing to me, is nothing but a 'fine detail' to you? You're despicable.'

'Despicable now? As well as a liar, two-faced? Well, it's better to find out sooner than later what you really feel.' Unlike Caitlin, he had not resorted to sarcasm. His words appeared to be spoken with a sincerity that amazed her.

'Anyone who can keep up this charade deserves an Oscar.'

He walked toward her, sudden menace in his measured stride. Roughly taking hold of her shoulders as she quivered with shock, he spoke in short, pointed words that shattered her for the second time. 'I don't love Patricia. That's rubbish. What's the matter with you? Are you psychotic with jealous delusions, or simply an insecure child?'

'Explain this!' She snatched up the bracelet and quoted the inscription that had burned itself into her brain. '*To My Beautiful Pattie*. Do you give such a personal gift to a woman you divorced seven years ago? What do you take me for, Will?'

With a gesture of disgust, he pushed her down on the bed and stepped back from her.

'A little spy thinks she's discovered my dreadful secret?' he said mockingly. 'As it happens, Pattie is my daughter.'

She did not believe him. He had never once spoken of having a child.

Why would he have concealed such an important piece of information?

'I don't have to account to you, Caitlin, but I will. We did have a baby girl, Patricia and I. It's why we married so young. Patricia was pregnant. Pattie stayed with her mother after the divorce. It pretty well broke my heart, but it was better for her. I only get to see her on holidays. That photo I keep is the only reminder of all the damage caused by our divorce. I missed her growing-up. She's turning sixteen next week . . . sweet sixteen.'

'You would have told me.' Caitlin felt as though a drug whirled in her bloodstream, making her giddy, making her arms and legs grow weak.

'I *would* have told you,' he confirmed. 'I was hesitant. I had no idea how you would react to having a step-daughter taller than you are. The age difference between us has been one thing I've worried about, when I was stupid enough to think we might have a future together.'

His cutting words had a horrible ring of fact. 'And then, I had to break the news to Pattie. I wanted to tell her in person that I intended to re-marry. I wanted her to accept you as someone I loved, someone I wanted her to meet with an open mind.'

Every word he spoke was in the past tense. The look he gave her left her in no doubt her suspicious accusations had hurt him more bitterly than she could ever imagine.

'You should have told me,' she whispered.

'No. It's shown me your true feelings. You're not a person I could live with. One day, loving, the next, jealous, insecure, full of doubt and accusation. You don't trust me. The fact remains, I can't trust you, either. It's no good, Caitlin.'

So they were parting. This was probably the last meeting they would ever have. She'd thrown away love, stamping it out when it was only a tender shoot, unable to withstand the hostility her fear had given vent to. Will was absolutely right about her. She had lacked faith in him and courage to handle her fears as an adult would. Rather than confessing her insecurity, she'd hurled insults and accusations at him. No wonder he'd backed off. There was nothing negotiable in his attitude as he stood by the door, waiting for her to leave.

'I'm sorry,' she began, but he interrupted, his expression fixed.

'Yes. I'm sorry too. I thought you and I . . . ' His mouth twisted in an effort at self-control. 'I'm going to call you a taxi. It's best if we call it a day.'

He turned on his heel and walked out.

9

Moving as though in a dream, Caitlin stumbled from the room. She could hear Will on his mobile, giving directions to the taxi company. Jackie and Katy lay curled up in the spare room. They were hard to wake and reluctant to go with Caitlin when she explained they were going home. Katy was almost sleep-walking, while Jackie sat in a sulky silence as Caitlin packed up their toys and clothes. She had no idea how she would make her way down the steep block of land in the dark, with two semi-conscious children. Somehow practical details seemed irrelevant.

Will sat stiffly on the sofa where, not long before, they had exchanged tender kisses. Now he looked as remote as a judge about to pass a heavy sentence on some transgressor of the law.

It was too late to attempt a reconciliation with him. Too much had been said. Fate had dragged their fears into dazzling close-up. They had seen each other's hidden natures too clearly to ever go back to the superficial pleasantness of first acquaintance. And she couldn't deny that Will's assessment of her was right. She *was* wary, she *was* afraid to love again, and that fear had successfully destroyed her dearest dream. Just as Will had turned on her when she revealed the facts of her past affair, so she'd rejected him — accusing him, judging him, creating this alien stranger who waited coldly for a taxi to remove her from his life forever.

If only he'd told her about his daughter! That must be why he was rushing off to Melbourne.

She could understand his delicate position. He'd wanted to present Pattie not with a *fait accompli*, but with the option of agreeing to her father's wish to marry again. His romance with Caitlin had been so swift. A few weeks ago she hadn't existed in his life. Since then, their meetings had been strange, keyed-up times — hardly the right setting for calm discussions about a future neither had made a commitment to. They'd triggered deep-buried defenses in each other. She'd been moody and suspicious. Will had behaved just as strangely. Only powerful attraction had forced them to persist. Letting go of the past had dredged up too much regret, too many bad memories. Neither of them had been able to deal with those feelings.

As she stood waiting for the cab, tears spilled and ran down her cheeks. In this house, Will had cooked her meals, given her a massage, made her feel special, nurtured, cared for. When he'd given her an engagement ring, she'd thrust it away like a venomous spider. If only one could undo misjudged actions and un-say cruel words! Oh, now she wanted to tell him she loved him. Barely ten minutes ago, his face would have shown her the joy those words meant to him. It was too late now. Painful as it would be to leave, she wished the taxi would arrive.

He was standing stiffly, as though on guard, as she walked up to him.

'I suppose you want me to take Charley? Will they allow him in the taxi?'

Will eyed the dog who, sensing the troubled atmosphere, wore an anxious expression as he stared from one stranger to the other.

'There's no reason to make his life a misery, just because we're breaking up. He can stay.'

'Thank you.' A small sob escaped her as the vulnerable existence of the unloved creature seemed too much to bear. Love and kindness were so precious, but why were they so rare? She stood irresolute until the taxi gave a toot, and Will stepped forward to lift Katy into his arms and sling the carry bag over his shoulder.

'You help Jackie,' was all he said.

He saw both children safely buckled

into the safety belts and waited for Caitlin to step in beside them. He dropped the bag on her lap and firmly closed the door as she gave instructions to the driver. He did not acknowledge Jackie's sleepy wave. He had already disappeared into the darkness.

At home, robot-like, Caitlin settled the girls and sat staring into space. Scenes kept flashing in front of her eyes . . . Will's loving expression changing to shock when she flung his offer of marriage across the room . . . His stony expression while she accused him of falseness and lies. No man could forgive such insults. She'd known that, but the words had spilled out, regardless, as though she wanted to condemn herself to unhappiness. Why? With Richard, she'd taken such care to be calm and rational, no matter how bitterly she'd resented her position. He would have been astonished to hear her hurling abuse, making demands, bursting into tears. Had she thrown at Will all those unexpressed feelings for another man who was long gone from her life?

* * *

After a night of little sleep, she still felt numb. She'd thrown away her last chance with Will. He'd made that plain. How vividly she could see the hurt on his face and hear his adamant words. All she could do now was make her plans for the coming days. Heather and Tony would be home soon. In less than a fortnight, she would have to take up her return ticket home. It was unlikely she'd see Will again. She had to accept that he was gone.

Returning to New Zealand felt like exile. She needed her family. These last weeks had shown her living like a hermit was no answer. The little she'd seen of Australia had only raised her curiosity to see more of the unique continent so full of ancient landmarks and extremes. The flora and fauna were so exotic, and the climate so extreme, one could spend a lifetime gathering new experiences. A nurse could always get a job, but at present she was tied to a mortgage and long-term debt. To move to Australia she would have to sell her unit.

No, these random thoughts were just a subtle way of clinging to Will. Forgetting him wasn't going to happen. Even with the Tasman Sea between them, she would always remember what they'd shared. She must just get on with life, get the house spic and span for Heather and enjoy her last days with her nieces. The one bright thought in all her unhappiness was that Will had solved the problem of Charley. Picturing the dog in his new home, she managed a wan smile. The unwanted mutt had certainly wormed his way into her heart. For all the misery he'd suffered at the hands of humans, he had simply forgiven and accepted a new life. Had she been living here, she'd have happily given him a home. At least

Will would make sure he was never ill-treated again.

Will had seen her at her most childish — worse than Katy throwing a screaming fit in the supermarket. He could reach that hidden part of her nature, just as he could reach her opposite, joyful side. They'd raced along the beach and splashed in the shallow tide on New Year's Day. They'd played in the tumbling breakers like ecstatic children. She'd never let herself go like that with any man. Some of her moments with Will had held such peaceful certainty, such an ease that felt so right. Pain slammed into her and she pressed her face into the pillow, wanting to muffle her sobs.

She went about the usual domestic routine, pushing away the image of Will boarding a Melbourne-bound plane. Jackie and Katy were starting to ask when their parents were coming home. After Heather's regular phone call, a fight erupted, which ended in tears and tantrums. Caitlin found she was short on patience, and snapped crossly while the girls stared with large, accusing eyes, wondering where their indulgent aunt had gone.

It was only fair to tell them what had happened.

'I'm sorry,' she said. 'I shouldn't be angry with you because you disagreed. Will and I had a really bad fight too. That's why I'm sad. He doesn't want to see me anymore.'

Jackie and Katy seemed to understand that even in the adult world, people fought and felt unhappy. They played together amicably and did not make demands, but Caitlin hardly noticed. By organizing the next days into blocks of time when she shopped, tidied the house and played with the girls, she found she could numb painful feelings. Perhaps she was in shock. After a few days, a screen dropped between herself and the world. Losing Will seemed dull and distanced. She could not share the girls' excitement that their parents would soon be home. She sat through television comedies without a smile. News items of family tragedies or global disasters could not reach her compassion. She tried to believe she really didn't care.

When Martin called up, Caitlin invited him round to dinner. He was good with children, and would relieve some of the pressure on her. It wasn't hard to guess who he wanted to talk about. Angela had turned down his invitation to partner him to the masked ball.

'She said she hadn't decided whether she wanted to go, but I think she's waiting for someone else to ask her.'

He talked on and on about the possibilities and repercussions of this setback, while Caitlin barely restrained her irritation. People in love were obsessive. They could think of nothing and no one but the person they'd set their attention on. All the time Martin speculated, Caitlin wanted to tell him about herself and Will, but Martin was the wrong person to confide in. He regarded her as a wise guide. The idea of being the muse of love almost made her laugh. If he could have witnessed her performance on that dreadful night, he surely would remove himself to consult some other oracle.

'Anyway, she said 'No',' Martin repeated for the tenth time.

'Then you must simply go with someone else.' She spoke in her most practical voice. 'Let's have a game of snap with the girls.'

'I don't know who else to ask.' He could be dogged. 'What about you?'

'*Me?*' She had no desire to go to any social event without Will.

'You might not have a partner?' He certainly made it plain he would prefer Angela's company. Unfortunately, his words were true. Heather and Tony intended to go to the ball as they were organizers. Valentine's Day was a highlight on the society's calendar, and she guessed the ball would be the main topic of conversation during the rest of her stay. If she cut herself off and showed no interest, she would only seem rude. Will wouldn't be there. She doubted he would hurry back from his Melbourne visit simply to attend a social function.

'Oh, why not?' she said indifferently. 'I warn you, I won't be much company but we may as well go together. It's better than arriving alone. Once we're there we can split up and mingle. That's one thing about just being friends.'

He looked pleased. 'I wish every girl was as sensible as you.'

She nearly laughed as she shuffled the pack. Trying not to show how bored she was, she began to deal.

* * *

It was the day of Heather and Tony's homecoming. *Welcome Home!* banners fluttered above the doors, and the children were red-cheeked and restless.

'When are they coming?'

It was the twentieth time Caitlin had

answered but she said patiently, 'Soon, darling. It depends if the plane arrives on time.'

But the girls had no sense of future or postponed events. Katy stamped her feet while Jackie wept. 'I want Mummy and Daddy *now*.'

'Soon, Jackie. Soon.' Trying to distract the pair kept her so busy she wasn't expecting to hear the slam of the taxicab door. The girls raced down the path to the gate, Caitlin following. Heather looked relaxed and tanned in her tropically-bright dress covered in flower and fruit designs. Tony had lost that harried expression of a man swamped by pressures. Vying for attention, the girls demanded hugs and kisses until finally Heather disentangled herself from her daughters' clinging arms and embraced her sister.

'You'll never know how good this break has been, and we owe it all to you.'

Caitlin felt a glow of pride. In the short space of Heather's absence, she'd changed from being single and uncertain of the ways of parenting. Now she realized there were no perfect answers. You just went with the flow, day by day, learning and growing just as much as the children.

Inside, she'd prepared cool drinks and snacks for the travelers, before they insisted on producing gifts and souvenirs the excited girls pounced on.

'And this is for you.'

Tony was offering a jewelry box. Somehow dreading the gift, she slowly opened the lid and saw a dainty silver bracelet, engraved with the single word, *Caitlin*. The coincidence was just too much and she was flooded by memories of the night she'd lost Will because of a jealous misunderstanding. The innocent token of thanks gleamed in her hand, a modern piece, not really like Will's exclusive choice for his daughter Pattie, yet close enough to remind her what she'd wasted and thrown away.

Tears spilled from her eyes. Horrified that she was putting such a damper on the homecoming, and realizing she must seem ungrateful and strange, she turned and rushed from the room, searching for somewhere private to let her emotions escape. But Heather followed, understanding the upset had to do with Will. She tapped and entered the bedroom where her sister was lying facedown, sobbing. Heather sat on the edge of the bed and gently stroked Caitlin's dark auburn hair.

'I'm sorry. I didn't mean to spoil your homecoming.'

'Don't be silly. Can you tell me what's happened?'

'Not now. Later. I'm all right. I've been stupid. I've ruined everything.'

'It's Will, isn't it?'

As Caitlin's tears flowed faster, Heather just sat quietly, passing tissues from the box beside the bed.

'Do you want to talk about it?'

'No.' Caitlin's voice was muffled. 'Not now. Please just leave me alone. The girls have been waiting all day for you.'

'I'll come back later.' Heather's tone was full of sympathy as she left, and Caitlin could hear the murmur of concerned voices in the adjoining room.

She sat up, sniffing and wiping her wet cheeks. Heather and Tony had no idea how deeply she'd fallen for Will. This was no light holiday romance. She'd never been the type to flit from partner to partner. Her heart was sincere and deep in its attachments. Once she'd given her love, it was a lasting state. Even as a child, she'd been inconsolable when she had to change schools and lose former friends. Her mother's early death had been a dreadful blow. She knew her intense affections had sometimes worried her older sister. Heather had stepped in and tried to guide her through her adolescence, but even now the risk of being abandoned felt too painful to bear. Had she carried the same fears into adult life? Without knowing it, perhaps she drove away the people who might want to love her.

She'd certainly succeeded in doing just that to Will.

* * *

Saint Valentine's Day was less than a fortnight away.

Tony wasted no time in moving into action for the society's prime annual function. He was a born organizer, able to enthuse volunteers by turning chores into a kind of group party. His persuasion had members stepping up with offers of entertainments, food, drink and general assistance. He had a sense of theatre, acting as pseudo-producer of the event, instinctively knowing the right person to ask when help was needed. Witnessing several impromptu meetings at the house, Caitlin thought the society was lucky to have her brother-in-law at the helm. It could not help but be a success. If only she could feel involved.

Heather and Tony tried to interest

her, suggesting various costumes and masks. Caitlin stood like a statue while her sister draped her in silks and satins, pinning shoulder tucks and skirt gathers in the folds of her improvised garments. Heather was clever with needlework and design. Guided by her astute eye, a scrap of lace, cheap belt or necklace could work a transformation.

'Paper masks are too ordinary,' she said, answering Caitlin's listless question. 'I've borrowed a library book on mask-making. I'm going to create papier-mâché designs to suit what we wear.'

But the fun of assuming the dress and manners of a past age escaped Caitlin. While pins flashed and scissors snipped, she remembered her introduction to the society, and the whirl of emotional excitement at her first meeting with the Prince of Lochac. That was over. She'd agreed to go to the ball with Martin. Hiding her despondent feelings, she joined in the painting of the masks, pretending an interest she did not feel. Heather knew her sister well enough to see she was heartbroken, but did not probe.

The best way to deal with Will's disappearance was to keep busy. The planning of costumes was underway, and some of the cooking was elaborate. The committee wanted a centerpiece for the main table — two swans with necks intertwined — and the mechanics of construction had everyone chipping in ideas. Heather drew a blank after turning out her kitchen cupboards. Tony experimented with plastic and rubber inventions in his garage. But try as they might, the marzipan would not stick to the slippery surfaces and the pitiful swans had them in fits of laughter. Never had less romantic birds courted on a festive table.

The problem was finally solved after Caitlin spent an hour dipping her hands in the papier-mâché bucket. Two presentable if rather stiff-necked birds sat drying in the afternoon sun, awaiting their icing, gilding and feathers.

Martin was noticeably absent. Caitlin guessed he'd had second thoughts about his invitation. After all, they had no romantic link, and he must hope Angela would change her mind. There was no opportunity to ask him if he would prefer they each go alone. The one time he visited, he wanted to see Tony and barely acknowledged Caitlin. Yet her heart almost stopped when she overheard them make a casual reference to the duties of the prince. Surely they knew Will had left Sydney? Presumably some other prince would have to stand in for him on that most romantic of all nights. Unless Will had returned?

Anticipation and dread combined to make her feel quite ill. She'd been so sure they would never meet again. To arrive at the ball and see him there would be more than she could cope with. Could she get out of going? It was too late. Heather would be really offended, especially after her hours of patient sewing.

She had created a pink silk gown, full-length and very low-cut, scoffing at Caitlin's complaint that she hadn't a voluptuous figure to fill out that style of bodice.

'We'll just pad out your bust,' she'd said. Caitlin's mask was to be a rather sly-looking cat's face, with elongated eye slits, a retroussé nose and arched cheekbones. Tony was wearing a Celtic costume and a horrible Druid's face that sent Jackie and Katy screaming in mock terror from the room whenever he tried it on. The girls had pretty frocks and simple silver-paper party masks. Heather refused to tell anyone what she planned to wear.

'The one thing I can promise is that you'll never recognize me,' was all she would say.

Despite her sadness, Caitlin was enjoying the companionship of family life. When she'd been in sole charge, it had been a lonely and responsible time.

It was good to hear Tony's energetic footsteps stamping down the hallway, good to smell Heather's tasty cooking and see clean clothes flapping in the breeze. Such everyday routines helped take the edge off her pain.

Tony had to return to work and Heather was busy organizing school and pre-school arrangements. Caitlin's stay had almost run its course. After the ball, she would say goodbye and return to her empty unit. Funny, she felt she'd left that life behind. So many hopes and possibilities had flowered here. The old routines felt dead. She felt no sense of loss over Richard, not even resentment now. Will had healed the past for her. She hadn't been able to see that until it was too late.

* * *

The day before the ball, Caitlin knew she could not put off her departure any longer. She checked the internet and booked the first available return flight, just three days away. The chore of packing remained. Why was it that suitcases seemed to shrink? She hadn't bought many things — a few souvenirs, Martin's table mats from the zoo, the special pictures the girls had done for her. Heather found her sister struggling like an overweight woman trying to fit into a petite sized dress, as she packed and re-packed her case.

'What's this?' She'd picked up Caitlin's horoscope.

'Just something I tossed in. I went to see an astrologer and she spun me such a good tale I decided to bring her predictions with me.'

'Mind if I read it?'

'If you want to. It's full of promises. Romance, travel, happiness . . . '

'Sounds at least partly true.' Heather sat on the edge of the cluttered bed and gently raised the topic of Will. 'You know, I wish I hadn't been so negative about Will when you first asked my opinion. It wasn't fair to him, and I think I made you wary.'

'No, it wasn't you. After that affair in New Zealand, I wasn't ready to trust any man. I took every little thing the wrong way.'

She told Heather the story of Angela's supposed engagement and her jealousy over the inscription on the silver bracelet.

'It was a two-way problem with communication,' Heather reminded her. 'Will put you on a pedestal. He was very judging when you decided to be honest with him.'

'If I hadn't been so uptight, we could have just enjoyed ourselves.'

'It's not that simple. Remember before I married Tony? Even on the eve of the wedding, I was in a panic. I was going to call the whole thing off. It's natural to have doubts.'

Caitlin burst into tears. 'I love Will! We could have been engaged. Instead I threw his ring away. He's a kind man. He even gave Charley a home.'

'Who's Charley?'

Between her sobs, Caitlin explained

the story of the unwanted dog.

'I'm glad Will's taken him. I used to worry about that poor animal. At least he's got a second chance at happiness.'

Caitlin was slowly calming down, but now she'd started talking she could not seem to stop.

'Why did we argue and fight? We seemed to do nothing but disagree.'

'Nothing else?' There was a teasing note in Heather's voice. Caitlin was silent, remembering the sensual caresses and persuasive kisses that had swept away her self-control. How tempted she'd been to give herself completely to the man who fired her with desire.

Heather sighed. It seemed hurt feelings, fear and pride were stronger than the romantic endings of fairy tales. She remembered the message Martin had asked her to pass on.

'I forgot to tell you. Martin phoned. He's sorry to disappoint you, but he can't partner you. Seems Angela's had a change of heart. He's taking her to the ball.' She decided to leave out the details of Martin's plan to fill his car with dozens of red roses. Fortunately, Caitlin did not seem at all upset by the news.

'We weren't suitable people to partner each other. I'm glad he's taking Angela.'

'But it leaves you without an escort.'

'I don't mind. There's only one man I'd want to go with. And he won't be there. I'll never see him again.'

'You will tomorrow. I wasn't sure whether to mention this, but Will intends to carry out his duties at the ball.'

Caitlin's pulse was racing. If Heather was right, the warning would give her time to cope with the shock of seeing Will again. 'Are you sure? Will's in Melbourne. Didn't you know?'

'He's back.'

'When?' She was trying to hide the hope that surged through her heart.

'About a week ago.'

A spasm of pain compressed Caitlin's lips. 'He hasn't been to any of the meetings here.'

'He said he'd rather not come here at present.' It was Heather's kind way of saying he was avoiding Caitlin. But nothing could soften that message, though Heather placed a comforting arm around her sister. 'Do you want to opt out of going tomorrow?'

Caitlin edged away. 'His loss, not mine.' She set her features in a cold, proud mask. No way was she going to fall apart and refuse to go to the Valentine masquerade.

10

Overexcited by the ball preparations, Jackie and Katy lost their appetites and begged to try on their dresses until Heather insisted they have a rest.

'Otherwise you won't be allowed to go.' Ignoring their protests, she sent them to their room. But the cry of dismay Caitlin heard from her sister had nothing to do with the children.

'I can't believe this!' Heather was struggling with a zip that could not be persuaded to cover her expanding waistline. 'I look like the 'before' advertisement for a weight-loss clinic.'

'Let me try.' But the problem required more than brute strength. Heather's pregnancy had reached one of those growth spurts and she looked as though she'd advanced by a couple of months, rather than two weeks.

'I feel like an over-stuffed sausage

casing in these breeches. And the waistcoat doesn't even meet in front.'

'So you were going to be a man tonight?' Tony grinned as he eyed his wife's swelling bosom. 'I don't think you'd fool anyone, sweetheart.'

She smiled back, slapping his wandering fingers.

Caitlin had realized how to overcome the problem. 'We'll swap costumes.'

'But you look so pretty in the dress I made.'

'I'd like to dress up as a man. It would be fun. Anyway, my dress is too big. You won't need padding!' The idea of masquerading as a man appealed. The sleek breeches, elegant ruffled shirt and elaborate waistcoat would look good on her slim figure. She would have the added satisfaction of seeing Will look around in vain for her, while she could observe him behind her disguise. She'd been dreading that awkward moment when, inevitably, they would recognize each other and have to act as strangers.

Heather was delighted by her reprieve. With a few adjustments the pink silk dress fit, its full skirt accommodating her in a flattering way and its plunging neckline drawing attention to her voluptuous figure. Some pins and tucks made her sister's costume equally satisfactory. She brushed Caitlin's hair back smoothly, in the style of a dandy, fastening it at the nape of her neck and applying a special lightening powder. The brocaded waistcoat buttoned snugly over the loose shirt, and the emerald-green satin breeches showed off her narrow hips and well-shaped legs.

She was at a loss to find suitable shoes and stockings, as the breeches finished just below the knee. Heather quickly sorted out some old white pantyhose, and found two garish gilt buckles to adorn the front of Caitlin's court shoes. Both sisters tried on their masks. Caitlin was pleased to exchange her cat mask for Heather's simple black velvet design. She suspected the papier-mâché of the more elaborate model would become hot and uncomfortable as the night wore on.

Tony looked truly evil in his short sack-like tunic and hideous mask. He pranced about the room, pretending to attack the women and carry them away. By now, the children had escaped from the bedroom and ran about, screaming at the fun. Caitlin found she was suddenly looking forward to the ball. She remembered the start of her holiday on that night when fate had introduced her to Will.

Scenes swirled in her mind — the beaches, the cozy tea-shop, the country cottage, Will's house by the sea. His face in its clear-cut handsomeness, its tenderness, anger and confusion, appeared in front of her. The memory of his hands and persuasive lovemaking made her dizzy, until she withdrew quietly to her room. Facing Will would be the hardest thing she'd done in a long time. Without her disguise, her feelings would be transparent. Would he stare at her coldly? Ignore her? Treat her with the aloof contempt she deserved?

He'd certainly seen the worst side of her nature; a side she'd hardly even known about, a dark, hidden aspect of her soul. She'd been jealous, accusing, and sarcastic. No wonder he'd refused to come to the house. Perhaps he hated her.

She wondered what had happened during his Melbourne visit. She would never know. Tears filled her eyes but she stood up determinedly. No use giving in to self-pity and regret. There was a ball to go to. She checked her appearance, liking what she saw. A young and stylish dandy, elegantly clad and sleekly coiffured, gazed back from her mirror. Will would need more than sharp eyesight to recognize her tonight.

* * *

A feeling of déjà vu marked the journey to the hall in Tony's run-down van.

The car park was already lined with vehicles, but the only one Caitlin searched for was not there. Relief and disappointment jostled in her emotions as she climbed from the van, brushing scraps of potato chip and fluff from her costume. Heather struggled to the ground, complaining she felt like an elephant, but looking very feminine in her flowing dress. Music drifted from the lighted doorway. Inside, a kaleidoscope of colorful costumes turned the hall into a magical world of fantasy.

There were no particular rules tonight as to what might be worn. Some members had dressed in medieval style but others had elected to come as animals, nursery-rhyme characters or peasants in national dress. A tall figure in a gorgeous variegated suit had completely blackened his face and made up his lips with thick white paint. A leopard-spotted furry shape skittered up to the new arrivals, tipping its bewhiskered face this way and that, patting the children on the cheek with velvet paws before prancing back to join the crowd. A filthy-looking beggar wearing rags sidled along behind them, pretending to pick their pockets. Tony threatened to cast an evil spell on him, at which the beggar scuttled off, Tony in hot pursuit.

Elegant courtiers conversed and flirted in select groups, ignoring the rabble of woodsmen, peasants and gypsies. A tinker tried to sell his spoons and saucepans, his costume clanking and rattling as he walked. The girls looked on, astonished at the transformation of sensible grown-ups.

Caitlin sensed that Will had not yet arrived. She would know, whether he came as a prince or in disguise. Martin, dressed as a page, entered the hall with a tiny but shapely princess by his side. So this was Angela, complete with golden ringlets, a rhinestone diadem and rosebuds scattered on her white gown. No wonder her escort was smitten. Angela was a picture of loveliness and Martin's costume suited him. Together they looked a well-matched pair. As she smiled up at her partner, Angela showed no desire to be on anyone else's arm. Perhaps true love might yet conquer her flighty ways. Caitlin's own hopes might be dead, yet she was pleased to see Martin walk tall and proud with his lady love.

Will appeared just then. She recognized him instantly, despite his dashing highwayman's attire of swirling cape and tight breeches. He carried a firearm in his hand and a black silk handkerchief concealed the lower half of his face. He looked both dangerous and romantic, a man who would stop at nothing to have his own way. Her heart was pounding steadily as she stayed back in the crowd, struggling with her emotions. They were as shattered as the first night they'd met. Why did he have this effect on her? Gazing at him, she longed to run across the room and throw herself into his arms. He was scanning the assembly as though searching for someone until he moved to join the crowd, his posture conveying disappointment. Had he been looking for her? Despite the finality of their break, surely this night of all nights must be reminding him of their first meeting, and all that had happened since?

Tony signaled his family group to follow him to a vacant table. As she followed, Caitlin had to force herself to look away from Will. He was now being absorbed into the gathering, where everyone seemed intent on playing their roles to the full. She had to remember this was all a game.

'Go and ask one of the girls for a dance, Caitlin.' Heather sank down on a wooden bench, slipping off her shoes.

'I can't dance with a girl!'

'You have to join in and play your part. Don't be surprised at what you see tonight.'

'I don't know how to act like a man.'

'I'm sure you do! This is the one night of the year when people can try on different disguises. It's theatre!' She was laughing now at Caitlin's reserve. 'If you choose a male partner, you'll trigger off suggestive jokes. Go on! What about Angela?'

Heather's words were interrupted as the hand of a lecherous old courtier descended on her plump shoulder. He wore a huge padded tunic with leg-of-mutton sleeves that made him look like Henry the Eighth, and behave like him too, for the bewhiskered old roué was eyeing her revealing neckline. Heather simply tossed her head and appeared to be enjoying herself. As she was led away to the dance floor, Caitlin shrugged and walked up to a quiet-looking girl dressed as Bo-Peep.

'Would you care to dance?' Deliberately she deepened her voice and stepped out with her shy partner. Bo-Peep wasn't much of a dancer, fortunately, and quietly shuffled around the floor following her partner's uncertain lead. To Caitlin's surprise, she began to draw out the nervous girl with a few flattering remarks such as she guessed a dandy would have recourse to make. Heather was right. It was fun to slip into a part and let imagination take over.

But she could not keep her eyes off Will. Every attractive female drew his attention and he was meeting no resistance, judging by the fluttering lashes and flirtatious gestures. He was certainly a handsome villain. One quick-thinking lady managed to faint into his arms, looking slyly pleased as the highwayman had to carry her to the sidelines to revive.

Several times, he stared at Caitlin reflectively, but he had not broken her disguise. To confuse him, she placed an arm around Bo-Peep, pretending to whisper in her ear. In fact, she was suggesting they should vacate the dance floor and find a cool drink. Wenches were handing out lemons stuck with cloves — a peculiar refreshment, used in a game of romance where kisses were stolen. Lemons were offered and taken, a clove being removed each time a kiss was claimed.

Now Will was presenting his lemon to the fainting lady, who instantly cast off her vapors and bestowed an ardent kiss as the game allowed. Furious, Caitlin snatched Bo-Peep's fruit, kissed her firmly on the cheek and hurriedly passed the lemon to Heather, stopping herself from presenting it to a handsome cavalier.

'Thank you, young sir,' simpered Heather, kissing her sister.

Saint Valentine was working his annual magic. Courting couples retired to the darker recesses of the hall. Flirtatious laughter and games took over from formal dancing and a few partners moved toward the privacy of the outdoors. Caitlin nibbled at cake and helped herself to mead placed strategically on the trestle tables. Feeling daring, she walked past Will, bumping him as though by accident. She merely nodded and walked past, wishing she could see his expression.

Surely he must sense her presence, even though she might not have recognized him if he'd dressed as a woman.

A moment later, she felt a tap on her shoulder. She turned and looked into the penetrating gaze of the highwayman. The silken handkerchief tied at the back of his head gave him the look of a determined rogue. His voice, as he addressed her, seemed to hold a note of insolence and veiled threat. Although she knew it was Will, her heart began a strange fluttering. He sounded so challenging as he spoke.

'Young sire, I have been watching you tonight. I do believe you have a valuable I am keen to take possession of.'

This was a game; of course it was. But how could she join in? If he heard her voice he would recognize her at once. Tossing her head, she turned to walk away, but felt a hard pressure against her spine and could not help the shudder that was both fear and anticipation.

'Sire, I repeat . . . a certain object

treasured by yourself is even more desired by me. This toy against your back will do no harm, unless my trigger finger should accidentally stray.'

She stood still, refusing to speak and give away her identity.

'You understand a highwayman's guise is excellent for gentle robbery? Therefore, my dumbfounded fellow, walk on to the door and walk speedily, for I am one pace behind and growing impatient for a little playful pillage.'

The game was too convincing. The quiet words no longer seemed like Will's. Could it be someone else? A genuine hold-up, carried out by a person with a grudge against the society? A fancy dress occasion would be the perfect opportunity to take some personal revenge, without the risk of identification. The toy against her spine, if it was a toy, felt real enough. She did not intend to run the risk of discovering it was a loaded gun.

Everything about the evening was so unreal that further unreality seemed quite normal. Her palms felt clammy and cold as she walked through the doorway, wondering how no one seemed to notice how the highwayman walked so close behind that she could feel his breathing on her neck.

Not noticing the beauty of the starry night, she could only feel the looming presence of trees surrounding the car park. The invisible figure on her heels directed her toward their heavy shadows.

'Keep moving, young fellow. Our business can be completed swiftly, so the sooner begun the better for us both. But you have not spoken a single syllable.'

Still she refused to give Will the satisfaction of unmasking her. For it was Will; of course it was . . .

'Yes, I have been eyeing you. Your waistcoat interests me. It conceals more than a sapling's skinny form. And what more clever place to conceal your treasures? Who would strip a young man of his finery in public? Those yonder trees would afford you the opportunity to divest yourself of your protection.'

A game! The tension was unbearable. She almost turned to tear off his mask, and hers. Somehow the suspicion that a stranger had copied Will's disguise and intended to harm her had lodged in her mind. Could this be some crazy rapist? Of course not! The hurts they'd caused each other were somehow transforming into overblown theatre. Her heart was racing. Was that from fear, or Will's closeness?

This was what happened at a masquerade ball. Heather had warned her everyone played up their roles to the hilt. It was true. She'd seen court ladies and gentlemen flirt and dally. Tony had raced about, frightening children out of their wits. That horrid beggar had wandered around scrounging food from people's plates. It was impossible to imagine they were ordinary people who would take off the masks and go home to suburban lives.

She'd felt like a young dandy, enjoyed the freedom and fantasy of her role. It had been fun flirting a little with pretty girls. But as the night closed around her and she was only a few inches from the tall man whose eyes were now invisible and whose voice sounded different from Will's, panic surged as two strong hands gripped her shoulders.

'Don't turn around.' He began to search her, running his fingers up and down her waist and hips and moving toward the buttons of her waistcoat.

'As I thought. Purses of uncommon value. You failed to take into account my special skill. My sixth sense, if you care to put it so.'

'Your sixth sense?' She had to break her silence and resolve this situation.

He was touching her and gently caressing her in a way she found arousing. Surely Will would not act this way, after all hope of their love had died? Desire and longing ran like a torrent in her blood. Confused, she cried out, 'No!'

At once the hands stilled. She heard Will's concerned tone.

'Caitlin? Have I frightened you? Surely you know it's me?'

Shaking all over, she pressed against him, unable to believe that he wanted this closeness after all that had happened. 'Yes, I know.'

'I had to speak to you alone. I realized you're about to fly back to New Zealand and I had to see you.'

'Why?' He'd gone out of his way to avoid her.

In answer, he untied his face covering and removed her mask. Full of uncertain words, explanations, apologies, sentences begun and half-finished, they tried to explain that the past was forgotten. Giving up the effort of language, their lips joined and they clung together as though nothing could ever pry them apart.

Their embrace was disturbed by the crunch of gravel as other lovers sought the shelter of the trees. Urgency filled Will's voice.

'Time's so short and we have so much to arrange. How long till you leave?'

'My flight goes on Tuesday.'

'You know what I'm going to ask, don't you?' Disregarding a passing couple, he took her in his arms again, their bodies melting unresistingly.

'Yes. And I know what I'll answer.' Her fears were gone. Her heart had opened itself again to love.

The rest of the evening passed in a trance-like mood of happiness. Will was required to propose a special Saint Valentine's toast to lovers, and to attend to other rituals expected of the elected prince. Before he went in to rejoin the throng, he pressed Caitlin to meet him at the close of festivities.

'You won't be home tonight. And don't worry about Charley. My neighbor's a dog fan. He's staying with her tonight.'

She promised to go with him. She would follow him anywhere now. With only two days left to think about their future, she would not waste a single minute.

Drawing her sister aside, she asked her not to mind when she did not come home with the family. Heather was understanding. The glow of love surrounded Caitlin as the pain of recent weeks was erased. The magic of Saint Valentine's Day was affecting many couples in the hall. Martin guided Angela on the dance floor as though in charge of a particularly rare and valuable work of art, and Tony had a wicked glint in his eye as he claimed his blooming wife from other suitors and led her away to some Druidic attentions she seemed only too willing to cooperate in.

* * *

Caitlin slid into the familiar comfort of Will's Porsche, not caring where they were going. What did the destination matter, when they were together? Kindly, fate had granted them an amnesty. How close she'd come to boarding that plane for a lonely departure, knowing she would never see Will again. How empty and painful her feelings had been.

She sat quietly as the car purred through the darkness. Sometimes they talked in bursts of confidences, or recalled the miserable days they'd spent apart. Will had seen his daughter and also visited his ex-wife. His voice sounded reconciled when he spoke about them now.

'Pattie's changed so much. She's always been my little girl. I suppose most fathers feel that way, and when you're living away . . . ' His pace had slowed, as though matching his reflective thoughts. 'I thought she'd always want my exclusive attention — resent me falling in love again. She just didn't mind. All she said was, 'As long as you're happy, it's fine by me.''

Caitlin did not point out that most teenagers would be far more interested in their own blossoming world of romance and conquest than in a distant father's plans. This was a touchy subject and she had no intention of repeating her previous mistakes.

'I'm glad you had a chance to talk.'

'Funny, we love each other but it was hard to think of things to say. It never used to be that way.'

He was struggling with the changing role she guessed all parents had to face. Caitlin reached across and touched his arm. She was offering comfort, but instantly felt the flash of desire. Will apparently felt it too. He took his hand off the wheel and reached across to smooth her satin-covered thigh.

'Did you see your ex-wife?'

'Only briefly. Again, nothing much to say. She's become a career woman. Seemed sure about where she's headed. And she's in a full-time relationship. Met the man, actually; a decent fellow. We got along okay.'

So his first love affair had served its time and had expired. Just like her relationship with Richard. After all the pain and misunderstandings, it was still better they'd cleared the air. If they'd refused to do that, half-buried memories were bound to have surfaced. At some time they would have worked their undermining harm. Now they could view their pasts as calm and peaceful tableaus, with no power to erupt and affect the present.

'That's good.' She moved closer and heard him murmur, 'I love you,' as though that was the only thing on his mind.

Judging by the speed and the regular flow of traffic, they must be on the freeway. Lulled by the gliding motion of the Porsche, she closed her eyes, breathing in Will's warm, familiar scent. Where were they? Really, she didn't care if he drove her to the ends of the earth.

Time stopped as she sank into a dream. Silhouetted gum trees flickered against the spangled night sky until the car made a sharp turn and appeared to enter a heavily-shadowed place. The sky's little lamps were extinguished and the wheels were turning on a stony surface now. Will slowed to a stop and pulled on the hand brake. He sounded quietly excited.

'Come on, hop out.'

She obeyed, standing beside the car, allowing her eyes to adjust to the darkness as Will switched off his headlights. He took her arm, guiding her as she stumbled on the rough path. The perfume of fresh country air was strong here. Rather an odd place to bring her, though now she was sure she'd been here before. The grassy scent was familiar, and she could smell roses.

'We came here before?'

'Indeed we did, my darling.'

Oh, she wanted these endearments! All her defenses had gone, along with her fears and doubts. That Caitlin was reborn as a grown woman ready to accept the joy that love could bring.

They seemed to be walking along an uneven brick path toward the cottage she'd so loved, but put out of her mind as one of those places she would never return to. Will must think this was a romantic place to propose to her, for she was absolutely sure he would ask her to marry him. Just as she knew she would give her answer with a glad heart. Yes, he was feeling about now for the key.

'If it's locked up, won't we be trespassing?' She thought someone might have bought the place and moved in by now. The last thing they needed tonight was any mishap.

'It would be trespassing, except the place belongs to me.' He did not hide the amusement in his voice. 'The legals are still going through but they've accepted the deposit. Settlement's in about a month.'

'But why?' Of course he'd looked at the place as an investment. He must be a business man through and through. Disappointment lanced her heart. So he planned to rip down the lovely little retreat to make more money? She wondered when he'd made his decision. Perhaps when their romance had died, he'd thrown himself into wheeling and dealing where the heart need not be involved.

'You're not pleased?' He still sounded teasing.

'I just wish . . . ' She could not finish the sentence. It was no time to criticize him and perhaps start another of their quarrels. If she loved Will, it would have to be the whole package, not some ideal version of him. And she did love him. She knew that without a doubt.

'Wish?' He wasn't going to let her stifle her words.

'It's just — I loved this little cottage. Of course I see it would be impractical to restore it. It would cost a fortune. I suppose the land's too valuable to waste on a run-down hideaway.'

'You still haven't told me what you wish.' He wasn't going to let this pass. She took a deep breath.

'I wish it was mine. Ours. I wish we could always be together. I wish this could be our special retreat, our own . . . ' Emotion overwhelmed her as he took her tenderly in his embrace.

'Wishes can come true. The cottage is yours. It's my wedding present to you. On one condition. Will you be my wife? Will you marry me and live with me and be my love?'

'I'll marry you! Of course I'll marry you!' Joy surged through her body as his lips found hers, sealing their promise before he opened the door and she stepped over the threshold. Expecting the mustiness of long neglect, she inhaled the surprising scents of linseed oil, lavender, and a hint of paint. A cleaner must have been here recently. As Will clicked on the lights, her gaze caught the gleam of polished floorboards.

'Surprised?' His chuckle gave away his pleasure.

'Did you do all this?'

'I could hardly bring my lady to a derelict cottage! Yes, I had permission from the agent to start work here last week. So far I've cleaned up, chucked out the old furniture, bought a new bed and fridge. I didn't want to go too far without your input.'

'Were you really so confident I'd say yes?' Was she on the edge of tears or laughter? He'd gone to an enormous amount of trouble, with no guarantee they would ever be able to repair their last quarrel.

'I hoped. I really hoped.' His arms came around her as he held her tenderly. 'And here we are.'

'Yes. Here we are.' She could not think about those past hurts and misunderstandings. Will was lighting candles in the small bedroom off the hall, where he'd left their bridal bed made up with soft white sheets, new pillows and a pale blue quilt. There was a fateful feel about this moment as Caitlin went to join him. Her life as a single woman was changing to a partnership. She and Will would be lovers. Her senses were fine-tuned as Will turned and pulled her close.

Unresisting, she pressed against him, responding to his musky scent and the thump of his strong heartbeat as his breathing quickened. This precious moment sealed their pact as one by one their garments dropped away and they stood skin to skin, shedding all masks.

Without hurry, they lay embracing, touching, exploring. Caitlin was grateful for this gentle build of intimacy. The extremes of the day and the totally unexpected shock of Will's proposal had drained her of nervous energy. She wanted to burrow against his solid body, grounding herself in his strength.

'Nervous?' He seemed to know she was on edge. 'This could wait, you know. We have all our lives ahead.'

'I'm fine. Just — blown away. Yesterday I was going back to New Zealand alone. Suddenly there was the masquerade ball, and you. This amazing cottage. Not to mention you asking me to be your wife!'

'Too much to process? Here, turn over, let me just stroke your back.'

She turned over and soon her secret smile acknowledged his knowing touch.

'Just what are you doing, Will?' She didn't need to ask, nor did he answer. With a sigh of pleasure, she gave herself up to the sensations flooding her body, and surrendered.

* * *

Caitlin awakened first. Shafts of sunlight glanced off the pastel wall and caressed her bare arm. She could hear birds calling in the tangled garden. Beside her, Will breathed steadily, his attitude one of deep rest. She gazed at him as he lay, naked and unguarded, and a swell of love flooded her heart. This aftermath of sexual desire bestowed its own blessing. How different from the way Richard had leapt from her bed, rushed off to wash and dress, and left her with a quick peck on the cheek. No, that was just another memory to discard. The past was gone. The future was unknown.

Here in this simple cottage she was replete with everything a woman's heart desired.

For a few minutes she simply drifted, reliving the roller-coaster she'd been on ever since she first landed in Australia. She'd arrived as a young woman convinced she wasn't ready for the responsibilities of marriage and children — would have laughed if anyone had suggested she'd be engaged within a month or two. Caring for her nieces had been a huge challenge, yet she'd succeeded. The love she felt for the two little girls enriched her. Even the thought of returning to Australia and being a permanent part of their lives filled her with incredible joy. Not only would she have Will as her partner and her friend, she would also be close to Heather and Tony, a member of a family again.

Will stirred and she reached over, stroking his tousled hair. His blue eyes focused while she smiled down at him.

'Good morning.'

'Good morning, my lady. I trust your repose was satisfying?'

'Actually, I was wakeful. A personage disturbed my rest, more than once.'

'Disturbed you?'

'Perhaps I mean, roused me.'

'I see. Like this? Or more like this?'

Caitlin's happy peal of laughter echoed through the morning quiet. 'Unhand me, sir!'

In daylight, lovemaking was slow and deliberate. Exploring, discovering, riding the waves of desire, they lost all track of time, finally falling into a peaceful sleep in each other's arms. Another hour passed before Will awoke and Caitlin stirred and stretched.

'I must have a shower,' she murmured, reaching over to caress his skin.

'I'll wait till you've finished in the bathroom. Meanwhile, I'll see to the morning repast. I stocked the fridge, fortunately.'

As he stood up, she indulged her gaze, liking his well-proportioned chest and lean hips as he pulled on his shorts.

'Take your time, my lady. Brunch will be served in the garden.' He bent and kissed her, lingering memories of intimacy shining in his eyes. When he left the room, she lay quietly a few minutes longer, savoring the fulfillment tingling through her body.

The small bathroom was basic, but Will had thoughtfully provided new towels and toiletries. While she stood enjoying the rush of warm water, her mind imagined the changes they would design together for their holiday retreat. Returning to her homeland now had a completely different agenda. She would sell up her assets, find another job in Sydney, and ask Will to help her decide on the best investment for her capital. He was an expert at making money. Sharing their mutual skills could involve many pleasurable projects in the years ahead. Already they had this cottage to re-design. She visualized changes they might make, even down to the details of restoration and decorating. Working side by side with Will would be the best part of the fairytale.

Wrapping herself in one of the large, fluffy towels on the rack, she wandered out to find Will. He had carried out a small table and was setting up their meal under one of the ancient fruit trees.

'Before we start, may I use your cell phone? Heather must be wondering.'

'Sure. It's by the bed, I think.'

The joy in her sister's voice when she heard Caitlin's news only added to the happiness of the day. But when Heather insisted they must have a celebration, Caitlin was jolted into the realization that in twenty-four hours' time she would be heading to the airport.

'There won't be time to plan anything,' she said.

'You don't know Tony! Make sure you and Will are back this afternoon. I can guarantee there'll be a party organized.'

Will was thoughtful as he watched her walk back to the orchard, her expression serious.

'You look downcast. Wasn't Heather happy about our news?'

'She was ecstatic! But I just wish I wasn't leaving so soon. I'm going to miss you so much.'

'That's a given for me too.' He beckoned, and gave her a comforting hug.

'You should have picked a local girl!'

'You're my girl. Even if you were an Eskimo.'

She managed a wan joke. 'At least I don't have to go to Alaska to wind up my affairs.'

'I'd be waiting for you, wherever you had to go. Now, are you ready to eat?'

He went to carry out the food — a simple repast of scrambled eggs, butter and toast, a gourmet marmalade and freshly-brewed coffee. As Caitlin looked around at the old cottage and overgrown garden, she knew she would always have this moment when she sat with her beloved, free from doubt, knowing she loved him from the very bottom of her heart.

* * *

Heather and Tony had conferred over the news, and decided to have an impromptu celebration. People would still be recovering from last night's festivities, a fact which did not daunt Tony in the least.

'We'll make it simple. A barbie with snags and tinnies on the back lawn.'

Heather smiled. She'd lived in Australia for years, but still found the casual slang entertaining.

'I'll get the girls ready, shall I? I guess we can just knock on doors.'

'Good idea. Let's go and spread the good news.'

But his wife thought it wasn't all good news. Her baby sister was leaving the next day and Heather knew how much she'd enjoyed Caitlin's company. The first week might have been rocky, but now they were closer than they'd ever been.

'It's such a shame they have to part tomorrow,' she said to Tony, who as usual had his flippant say.

'Absence makes the heart grow fonder.'

'Don't be too sure about that.' Heather's voice had a touch of asperity. 'Caitlin and Will are quite fond enough. Why do you think they've just become engaged? And I'm going to hate saying goodbye at the airport.'

'Your sister will soon be back.'

Her husband spoke as though selling up, packing, and receiving tax and emigration clearances were a mere trifle, but Heather disagreed.

'I don't think she has anyone to help her. I wish I could be there to lend a hand.'

Tony had heard enough negativity. 'She'll be fine. Now, let's load up the girls and get going.'

He hustled them into the van. In his opinion, Sunday was the perfect time to pay unexpected house calls. People might be asleep or having a lazy day. What better way to rouse them, than a cheery pealing of the doorbell?

The engagement was announced to a series of yawning, tousle-haired and bemused couples who found themselves accepting an invitation to an impromptu party. Revelers not yet recovered from the masked ball tried to drum up enthusiasm.

Back in the van, Tony sounded amused. 'They looked a bit pale!' He checked his address book for the next destination.

'Didn't you see how many jugs of mead were emptied last night? Perhaps people aren't ready for another celebration.'

Tony just laughed. 'We're not starting till this afternoon. Hours away!'

Heather just shook her head. His boundless energy never seemed to ebb.

They were passing a long beach, where powerful breakers reminded her of life's constant change. Overnight, her sister's future had reversed. She was about to marry, put down roots in a new country — perhaps have children one day with Will. How could things have changed so radically? Looking back, she saw the die had been cast on the night the Prince of Lochac walked across the room to meet the Lady Caitlin.

* * *

In her sister's home, Caitlin woke to the clamor of currawongs and kookaburras. She was leaving today. When would she hear those iconic Australian birds again? She lay reviewing the previous evening, which had been a raging success. When she and Will arrived, cars were parked on both sides of the road, and music rang out from the stereo. Tony had mowed the grass and a delicious scent hung in the still air. The girls ran out with their handmade *Congratulations* banner. Clapping and ribald comments suggested the guests had guessed correctly why the pair had arrived late.

The supper of sausages, barbecue sauce and bread was simple fare for an engagement party but nobody complained. Like the whining mosquitoes and grating cicadas, the food symbolized the casual outdoor life in Australia. People might tease her about her accent but she knew she was with open-hearted people who liked her. Yet so much had happened, and so quickly. She'd suddenly felt overwhelmed, and had slipped away to the shadowy porch. Will had followed, resting his arm around her shoulders as she'd leaned against him.

'Heather doesn't mind if you want to stay over tonight.' She'd longed to fall asleep in his arms, but he'd hesitated.

'There's something I have to reorganize, darling. I need to go home.'

The stab of disappointment hurt.

'You will come and see me off, though?' What a question! Yet again he'd hesitated.

'Yes, of course. But it's best if you go with Heather and we'll meet up.'

Whenever he reminded her he was a busy man with work to do, she was taken by surprise. But she knew the time for possessive doubt was over.

'That's fine.' She'd deliberately lightened her tone. 'We'll see you at the airport. Perhaps we should rejoin the party now.'

Apparently this was a side of Will she'd simply have to get used to. Perhaps all men could set aside their feelings when practical matters encroached? They'd said goodnight in the kitchen, in front of Heather, so there'd been no opportunity for close words. She reminded herself so many had been spoken — surely she had nothing to complain about?

Now she heard the patter of bare feet as Katy and Jackie arrived for their last morning cuddles with their aunt. The air felt thick with impending goodbyes as Caitlin reviewed the day's plan. Heather was to drive her to the airport in time for her pre-travel details, confirming her ticket, changing currency and duty-free shopping. Departure time was late afternoon, so allowing for the time change she would disembark in Auckland at eight o'clock. Ahead lay the massive task of emigrating. As well as disposing of job and house, there would be bills to pay, accounts to close, and the sorting and packing of her possessions. It would all take time and she had no one to help her.

Casting off her doubts, she stripped her bed, taking her sheets to the laundry where Heather was already sorting dirty clothes. A housewife worked every bit as hard as a nurse, without the weekly pay slip. Heather cared for her family out of love. Marriage and children were a full-time commitment when children were her nieces' age. The girls knew their aunt was leaving, and trailed after her, their mournful faces reminding her how deeply attached they had become to her.

'I'll soon be back,' she promised. Of course nothing could upset her plans. Surely not! Will would wave goodbye today, and in no time he'd be there at the reception barrier to welcome her back as his wife-to-be. She needed to hear his voice now. Loving words would ease the sadness of leaving. But the phone was silent. After breakfast, unable to restrain herself, she dialed his number. There was no reply.

'He's not there.' Unreasonably perhaps, she felt deserted.

'He told you he'd be busy this morning.' Sounding distracted, Heather was wiping up spilt juice and stripping off Katy's sun suit. 'I wish you'd be more careful, Katy.'

Heather was irritable today — her way of indicating she too would feel the wrench of parting from her sister. Caitlin had provided support, taking the girls for a walk, or reading them a story. Affable though Tony was, he always had such a full calendar of events, meetings and agendas that he could not be relied on to do domestic chores, except as a last resort. It was something Heather simply had to accept. Just as Caitlin had to understand Will would not postpone whatever business he was negotiating, in order to spend a last few hours with her.

No, she wouldn't let this mood prevail. He would meet her as he'd promised. She would enjoy these precious hours with Heather and the girls. Before she knew it, they'd eaten a light lunch of sandwiches and fruit and her sister was reminding her it was a long drive to the airport.

Once they were on the interchange to the airport, Caitlin scanned the traffic, hoping to catch sight of Will's Porsche. But there was no sign of him or his car, either en route or in the parking area at the terminal. How could she expect to spot it, among so many vehicles? Several times as they walked to the entrance, Caitlin thought she recognized Will, until a stranger of similar height or posture turned and faced her blankly. She fought back a sense of impending disappointment. How many times had their relationship nearly come to grief because she mistrusted him?

Ticketing and boarding queues were moving slowly through cordoned lanes. Heather was on alert as the girls scrambled over seats, dodged luggage trolleys and skidded on polished floors. It took the best part of an hour for Caitlin to complete her departure formalities, pay her airport tax and rejoin her sister.

'Surely this must be rush hour.'

Flight after flight filled the overhead information boards. Incomprehensible announcements were a background to the musical intonations of Chinese and Vietnamese travelers.

Turbaned men from far-off countries accompanied women draped in voluminous black garments. The smiles of solid-hipped Pacific Islanders hardly creased their plump features. Japanese gathered in orderly groups, absorbing information from tour conductors. Greeks and Italians gave way to emotional bursts of weeping as they embraced and kissed.

Among all the people, Caitlin searched for the one face she longed to see.

It was almost time to board. Her flight was creeping steadily to the top of the departure timetable. Her sister was trying hard to play down Will's odd absence.

'The crowd's so thick. Perhaps there was an accident and the road's been closed.'

Heather seemed worried, as though rumors about Will still bothered her. Caitlin could see she was angry that, at the last minute, he hadn't shown up. She was trying to maintain a brave face for her sister.

'I just know there's a good reason he hasn't come.'

But Heather sounded doubtful. It was Caitlin who had to reassure her, hugging her warmly.

'I've had a wonderful holiday. I can't wait to see you again soon.'

'No second thoughts?'

'I'm settling in Australia. Nothing will stop me.'

Hearing the conviction in her voice, Heather relaxed. With the girls in tow, they were making their way now toward the swinging doors beyond which only passengers were allowed.

Caitlin shuffled her tickets, passport and customs forms ready for inspection as the name and number of her flight sounded over loudspeakers.

'I have to go. When Will comes, please tell him I'm sorry we didn't get to say goodbye.'

Had Heather noticed the tears filling her eyes? She was relieved to pass out of sight through the passenger doors. Back in the waiting area, Heather could only gather her children and lead them over to the viewing windows to show them the departing planes lined up on the tarmac below.

The passageway seemed endless. Caitlin was not permitting herself to dwell on Will's non-appearance. She would never be able to think of any acceptable reason why he hadn't bothered to see her off. Yet she'd made a decision to trust him. There was no answer to her dilemma. Instead, she concentrated on her surroundings and the other economy-class passengers, now boarding according to alphabetical order.

International travel was exciting. Soon the inert aircraft would magically lift and soar into the heavens, defying apparent reason to cocoon its crew and passengers in air-conditioned comfort. Drinks would be poured and meals served. Music or a film would pass the time.

The world of travel had changed so much in one century. What progress would the next century bring?

A hostess pointed out her seat number, toward the rear sandwiched between a window and an aisle seat. A tall, good-looking man, traveling alone, it seemed, politely stood up to make room for her and helped detach her seatbelt wedged in the back of the upholstery.

‘Tried this airline before?’

He must be a regular commuter.

‘Yes.’ She did not explain she’d only flown once before.

‘Not bad service.’

Caitlin didn’t care about the service. The realization she was about to leave Australia and Will had just struck like a physical blow. Oh, why hadn’t he come? Why was she subjected to these continual tests of their love?

She pulled herself up. There would be an explanation. She mustn’t indulge in hurt or jealous doubt. She loved and trusted him. He’d never done anything to betray her. Yet she had to bite her lip to stop from breaking down and crying. The urbane man beside her, not sensing she was upset, was waffling on about duty-free shopping and rental cars. Soon she would plug in her headphones and apply herself to a concert program. No doubt he was a decent man, but she simply couldn’t be bothered making conversation with a stranger while her heart ached and her mind spun in confusion.

A vibration indicated the plane was taxiing toward the takeoff runway. Involuntary excitement flooded her body as the powerful craft gathered speed. The hostesses ceased their disaster management spiels and sat down. With a surge the plane lifted into the air. The change was so smooth she only realized they had attained altitude when the seatbelt lights were switched off and passengers began to move around the cabin. She was really going home. Her mind drifted, conjuring up Will's face. The image was so clear and warmed by such a loving smile she felt she was hallucinating.

Caitlin blinked. Yes, she really was staring up into Will's eyes as he politely excused himself to the man sitting beside her and bent across to speak. She was speechless. Her heart pounded with shock. If Will had wanted to surprise her, he had succeeded.

Was he really explaining to her fellow passenger that, should he be amenable to the exchange, there was a single seat available in Business Class, with all the extra amenities and service provided by the increased fare? Not averse to the offer, the man agreed to the swap, and Will eased into the vacated seat next to Caitlin, tenderly kissing away her tears.

'Hey, you didn't really think I'd let you go without a goodbye?'

She was clinging to his hand, as though still reassuring herself he was real.

'How?' was all she could say.

'I decided yesterday to try and get on the flight with you. I didn't tell you, in case it didn't work out. And I had to shuffle some work commitments, and arrange care for Charley. He sends you a big tail wag, by the way.'

'We'll share him, once we move in together.' Contented now, she rested her head on Will's shoulder, absorbing his reassuring warm male strength. 'Just one thing. Heather was really upset when you didn't show up.'

'Don't worry. I saw her, very briefly. I

thought I had plenty of time to buy a seat, but it was only by chance a late cancellation came up in Business Class. Very posh! They even boarded us by a different entrance.' He laughed, unable to hide his pleasure at the feat he'd pulled off.

But Caitlin knew his gesture was more than just a lover's playful surprise. He wanted to be at her side, to help with the practical tasks ahead and to reassure her she had a partner in every aspect of life. There might be words to tell him how much that meant, but for now she could not think of anything to say. Love and peace engulfed her. Sitting close beside her love, she allowed herself to float through this rarefied dimension toward her new life.

THE END

Other titles in the Linford Romance Library:

GIRL WITH A GOLD WING

Jill Barry

It's the 1960s, and Cora Murray dreams of taking to the skies — so when her father shows her a recruitment advertisement for air hostesses, she jumps at the chance to apply. Passing the interview with flying colours, she throws herself into her training, where she is quite literally swept off her feet by First Officer Ross Anderson. But whilst Ross is charming and flirtatious, he's also engaged — and Cora's former boyfriend Dave is intent on regaining her affections . . .

THE SURGEON'S MISTAKE

Chrissie Loveday

Matti Harper has been in love with Ian Faulkner since their school days. He is now an eminent cardiac surgeon, she his theatre nurse. Ian has finally fallen in love — the trouble is, it's with Matti's flatmate Lori! But whilst a heartbroken Matti prepares to be their bridesmaid, Lori is being suspiciously flirtatious with another man. How can Matti tell Ian without appearing to be jealous? Best man Sam Grayling tries to help, but only succeeds in sending things from bad to worse . . .